AF656927

Susp'ENDED

10 short stories

notionpress
.com

Susp'ENDED

10 short stories

Sudha Ramnath

notionpress.com

Notion Press

5 Muthu Kalathy Street, Triplicane,

Chennai - 600 005

First Published by Notion Press 2014

Copyright © Sudha Ramnath 2014

All Rights Reserved.

ISBN: 978-93-84049-62-1

This book has been published in good faith that the work of the author is original. All efforts have been taken to make the material error-free. However, the author and the publisher disclaim the responsibility.

No part of this book may be used, reproduced in any manner whatsoever without written permission from the author, except in the case of brief quotations embodied in critical articles and reviews.

Just building a car will not make it run. It needs 4 wheels. Same way this novel also has 4 wheels. My first wheel is my brother, VJ, who came up with this idea that I should write and publish a novel. My second wheel is my husband ... Ram who was my guinea pig and had to put up with listening to my stories, and the endless changes I made. My 3rd wheel is represented my kids... Sai, whose feedback on my stories was always waiting in my inbox and Kitty who yelled at me whenever I became lazy and was very vocal with her criticism. My 4th wheel is Notion Press for trusting in my ability to write.

I thank my 4 wheels.

Preface

I have always been thrilled by suspense stories. Whether novels or movies. Suddenly one day I thought, instead of being at the receiving end, can I give?

Foreword

The foreword is a strange literary beast. It introduces the larger work and / or the author – much as an emcee introduces a keynote speaker. For me, this is the first time that I am writing the foreword for a book written by someone, whom I know only through the hallowed portals of social media viz. the venerable Facebook!

Since early teens, the genre of detective, whodunit and mystery stories has never ceased to fascinate me. I was therefore, delighted when Sudha Ramnath chose me to write the foreword to her maiden linguistic foray in this domain.

Both the detective or mystery story is usually based on either analysis or deduction. The former was exemplified by Edgar Allen Poe and the latter by Arthur Conan Doyle through his evergreen Sherlock Holmes. Ofcourse you could always add the third mysterious unknown of intuition to this!

In modern times, the grand old Dame Agatha Christie wrote more than 70 detective novels as well as short fiction, writing well into her later years. Author of sleuth stories earned her titles like the "Queen of Crime" and the "Queen of Mystery."

The "Agatha Principle" is explained with this theory: "The least likely person is the killer, and no one is really who they seem."

Sudha, in this collection of 10 stories - both brief and large, with regional and ethnic subcultures - weaves in astute observations, dogged legwork, intuitive logic and perspicacious inferences with puzzling situations, supernatural elements and criminal minds.

You have it all here in this collection - stories with unexpected endings, investigations of a murder committed by one (or more) of a limited number of suspects, laws of natural justice, realism and imagery - dramatizing that crime can happen in one's own living room.

The Seed of Genius truly lies embedded within all of us until, like the cherry blossoms, it suddenly emerges forth. To me it is a simple vindication of this miracle of natural intelligences, which Sudha Ramnath ratifies once again with her Linguistic Intelligence.

I am confident that her 'maiden' work will inspire several others into expressing themselves.

ANKUR GUPTA

Author of "seeds of genius"

"All journeys have secret destinations of which the traveller is unaware."

Martin Buber

Contents

MISSION FAILED

A middle-class neighborhood in Delhi.

"Stop barking, Rover", said Neeta as she brought in the tea.

Naresh looked over his newspaper and asked, "Did Sheila go out?"

"Yes. Rover was barking his head off at her". Sipping her tea, Neeta looked at the growling dog. "I can't understand it. Ever since the day Sheila moved in as a paying guest, Rover has been unfriendly towards her".

"He is usually friendly. Wonder why he does not seem to like Sheila".

"Poor Sheila! She goes out of her way to be friendly with him. She is always trying to pat him on the head or trying to cuddle him. But the more she tries, the more he seems to hate her," Neeta observed.

"And Neeta, have you noticed the way he barks? When the kids irritate him, he sort of enjoys barking at them. This is different; a low growl from the back of his throat, as if he is scared of her".

"I know you are going to laugh at me, but even the money plant which Sheila waters regularly has wilted".

***

The kids were playing gully cricket and there was a loud shout when Umesh sent the ball through a window on the first floor.

"You should have been careful and not struck it so high. Now what will we do?" Deepak was worried.

"Last time, I was scolded when I went to ask for the ball. I am not going this time," said Umesh firmly, putting down his bat.

"Guys, the ball has fallen into Sheila auntie's house. She never yells at us like the others. So no worries. Umesh, go get it", Uday said.

Umesh was back in five minutes with the ball and a packet of biscuits. But he did not pick the bat and stood looking confused.

"What happened? Did she yell at you?" Deepak wanted to know.

"No. Not at all. In fact, she asked me my name and all about me. She was very friendly".

"Then why do you look so worried?" Uday walked up to Umesh…

"I can't understand it... I didn't like her at all. When she came near me, I felt like pushing her away".

"You know what? I didn't like her much too. Other aunties yell at us if we hit the ball into their houses. I can understand that. But this aunty goes out of the way to be friendly. But something in me makes me dislike her... don't know why," Uday said.

❖❖❖

The kitty party was in full swing.

"Angela, is this the new sari you bought from Bangalore?" Sanjana felt the fabric.

"Oh, yes! Isn't it lovely! It is pure Mysore silk".

"The combination of magenta and green is beautiful," Sanjana said.

"You should have worn the new pearl set you have with the sari," Asha suggested.

Meera came in bustling. "Girls, did you have the vadas which Mrs. Venkatesan brought over? They are delicious!"

"By the way, Meera, did you invite Sheila? She had particularly wanted to attend our parties in the colony," Asha asked.

Meera hesitated. "Hmmm... I actually planned to but somehow I didn't want her here. I know she is a sport; she offered to buy something, may be some ice cream, for the party unlike a few others who just cash in on others' generosity. But I am very uncomfortable in her presence."

"Did you find out anything more about her?" curiosity took the better of Sanjana.

"I asked Neeta and she too didn't know much. It seems she pays the rent on time, is a perfect tenant. No complaints of loud late night parties and boyfriends," Meera told the others.

Sanjana wanted to know where Sheila worked.

"Neeta didn't know. It seems when Naresh asked her, Sheila was very vague about it. Said she was a consultant.

She goes out at irregular times, doesn't have a car and takes the auto all the time," Meera had some details for her.

"Yes, I have seen her at the market sometimes. I did try talking to her but she seemed distant," said Asha.

"Neeta said it has been nearly a year since she became their tenant. And because Rover always barks at her, they have planned not to renew her contract. But when Neeta's mother-in-law had an attack last week, Sheila was very helpful and stayed with her all night. So now they feel indebted to her and may renew the contract," Meera went on.

Picking a *vada*[1], Sanjana said, "Yes, I remember. At that time, my mother-in-law also mentioned how sweet a person Sheila was and looked at me as if I was to take a lesson from her".

"Does at least she like Sheila then?" Asha gave voice to everyone's thoughts.

"Hmmm... Not actually. When Sheila tried to take my Pinky on her lap during the birthday party, I noticed my mother-in-law grab the baby and move away," Sanjana said.

Sighing, Meera said to herself, "Wonder what's wrong with Sheila! She is a perfect person in every way but no one likes her".

❖❖❖

---

1 *Vada* - A deep-fried ball of ground pulses, resembling a doughnut

Kunal took a swig from his mug of beer and pulled the plate of cashewnuts towards himself.

"*Yaar*[2], *I* was waiting for this drink from morning". There was silence until a few sips later.

"On my way to the pub, I saw this new girl... what's her name? Ah... Sheila!" Kunal smirked.

"And?" Rohit asked eagerly.

"I think she is easily available".

"You say that about every girl".

"But Rohit, this one has given me the invitation so many times with her eyes".

"Oh! Hey are you talking about Naresh's paying guest?" Gautam joined the conversation.

"Yes... the very same. Don't tell me she tried with you too!" Kunal was hoping otherwise.

"Of course she did," said Gautam.

More pegs were downed.

"You know what," Kunal's speech had begun to slur, "Some thing about Sheila is repulsive. Even if she wants me, I don't want her. I am desperate but even if she were the last girl on earth, I still don't want her."

"She is beautiful and has a wonderful figure. Seems like she is available. Then why don't we all like her?" Gautam looked into his drink for answers.

---

2 *Yaar* - Friend

Full of the philosophy born of alcohol, Kunal went on, "There is something unnatural about her. Some thing that makes her too eager to be loved; and this is what seems to put everyone off".

❋❋❋

Sheila sat in the balcony, staring into space. Breaking out of her stupor after a while, she grabbed her laptop and began typing...

We, the Martians, are technologically much ahead of the people on earth. But they have love, a concept we are not aware of. I was sent here to learn this emotion. I chose the Indian sub-continent as love is practiced in many forms here - towards animals, children, the aged and even towards plants. But I have understood that love can neither be taught nor be learnt. It can only be felt. I report a MISSION FAILED.

FREEDOM

I have liked very few men. The way things are moving now, I think I will end up hating the whole lot of them.

They don't know how it feels to be confined. I hate that. Even when mom tried to restrict me, I never listened to her. And now? These men have imprisoned me in a room. I, who had the whole world to myself and was the uncrowned queen, can now barely stand up in this cramped space. I suddenly feel movement under me. I am terrified. I stand up with great difficulty and look out of the small hole in the wall. We are sailing. With helpless rage, I limp back and lie down. The tears roll.

Memories of family and friends flood my soul and my heart wells up with sadness as we move further away from home. How easily I fell prey to their avarice! My mom had always warned me of man's selfishness but like all youngsters, I never gave it serious thought.

That day, I was with my friends and I noticed some strange men about. Their eyes spoke of undisguised greed. We became a little uneasy and were about to walk away when the men pounced on us. A couple of my friends ran away but help was not near and two of us were captured. I had tried to fight them off; I scratched at the face of one and bit another on his hand. But their brute strength overpowered us.

Now I wonder where my friend is. I had lost her in the scuffle.

They brought me in a jeep and loaded me into this boat under the cover of darkness.

❊❊❊

One of them stands before me. I note with grim satisfaction that he has bandaged his arm where I had bit him. He brings water and food and leaves it just inside the door and immediately locks it. Even though I am hungry and thirsty, I ignore it.

Suddenly, I sense several people watching me from behind the bars. They leer at my skin, my body, my youth. They speak in an unfamiliar language but I understand that I am going to be sold. I turn my back on them. I realise as long as I am on this boat, there is no escape.

❊❊❊

The door opens, waking me from my fitful sleep. From the sounds, I realise that someone has entered the room. I see a stranger with some food for me. He was not part of the group which captured me.

Something tells me he is not a bad guy. He murmurs soothingly and sits nearby, without trying to touch me. I slowly sit up and nibble at the food. All the while, he leaves me alone.

I learn to trust this guy and he too gets comfortable around me. He comes in with food and sits in another corner till I am done eating, watching me all along. I finish my meal and lie down in my place near the wall. From there, I watch him surreptitiously. He sits with his back to the wall and is lost in his thoughts. When he gets up to pick the food tray, he talks to me in his strange language. Though I don't understand a word, his presence comforts me.

He restores my faith in humanity and men.

❋❋❋

Once in a while, a few of the bad guys come stare at me and try to open the door. But the good one seems to be looking out for me. He yells at them to leave me alone and waits till they move away. Then he checks the locks as he murmurs those soothing words. What irony! The locks which are keeping me from escaping are also keeping me safe.

Months pass and we arrive at the destination. I see everyone buzzing about. Many new men clamber over and some of them are brought down to see me. I ignore them but this doesn't discourage them. They pass ugly comments and shake hands with my tormentors. A deal has been struck and I am sold.

Taken away from my home and family, I had found temporary safety and happiness in the kindness of the good guy. Now that is lost too and my fate is in the hands of my new masters. Misery.

❋❋❋

It is pitch dark when I hear keys being inserted into the lock. I watch the door open and the good guy tiptoes in, allaying all my fears. He quietens me down and gestures to go out with him. I follow him, in complete faith.

He helps me walk on a plank over to the shore. The fresh air feels so good after several months and I stretch to relieve my body of the many aches. I notice some tents and jeeps a little further away. Deep jungle lines the other side and he leads me towards it.

Oh! How wonderful it is to be home, back in the jungle where I belong. Without a glance back, I run to the green cover, slowly at first and with great speed as I gather confidence, all in the hope of finding a few fellow tigers.

MURDER AT SILVER OAKS

Olivia D'Mello threw her window open and stood there for a minute, taking in the cool breeze. She looked at the garden full of night blooms. She could see most of her tea estate, Silver Oaks, sprawling across the lush green hills of Ooty. She had feasted her eyes on this very scene, from this very window, for almost 40 years now.

The heady fragrance of the night blooms hit her and made her nostalgic about the bygone days.

She had come to Silver Oaks, as a shy, young bride. She bore two daughters and when they were still in school, her husband passed away. She learnt to run the estate on her own and went on to make it one of the best tea estates in Ooty.

A sudden gust of wind made her shiver. She felt her body ache and went to sit down on her rocking chair. As she slowly rocked, she continued to ruminate.

Her first daughter Pauline married Michael who was a friend's son. Michael, though not very rich, was very smart and worked for a software company in Chennai. Olivia had no problems with them. Devoted to each other, they lived a happy life with their son Mark.

But she was unhappy with her second daughter's choice. As soon as she saw Aaron, Olivia knew he was a wastrel, wanting to live a rich man's life without lifting a finger.

Sophie had met Aaron in Chennai, where she went to college, and married him against Olivia's wishes. Poor Sophie! Her dreams of everlasting love were shattered soon. She found that Aaron hated to work but loved money and he thought of her just as a source of easy money.

They too lived in Chennai, where Aaron had a small job, and only visited Ooty twice or thrice a year. But the visits were more than enough for Olivia. There were always demands for money and more money. It was either for their daughter Mary's school fees or Sophie's medical bills or the overdue house rent.

Olivia was well aware that part of the money always went into Aaron's pocket and was spent on drinks and women.

She got up to stoke the dying fire and came back to her rocking chair.

Fifteen years had elapsed after Sophie's wedding.

The sound of a car drawing up outside the bungalow disturbed her thoughts. Sophie stepped out of the taxi with Mary. Olivia rushed out to welcome them, but was shocked when she saw a bruised and teary Sophie walk past her outstretched arms, pulling 12-year-old Mary behind her.

It was evening and Olivia was sitting at her table, going through the estate accounts when Menon, their caretaker, entered hesitantly and said "Sophie *beti*[3] has not eaten any thing from morning." Olivia looked up from the notebook and said, "Leave her alone. Maybe she will be alright in a few days".

Menon, who had been with the family for 25 years, hovered around for a minute before saying, "We should not have let her marry that Aaron. Sarala and I never liked him".

Olivia put the pen down and smiled affectionately at him. "What to do, Menon? Every one is not as lucky as you and Sarala. Aaron does not care for Sophie as much as you care for your wife."

Just before going to bed, Olivia went into her daughter's room and sat next to her. Sophie, who was lying on the bed, turned towards her mother and held her hands and wept. Olivia did not ask her anything. She remained with her, stroking her hair, till Sophie fell asleep.

***

Mary was sitting on the steps, watching the ducks move around. Olivia went and sat next to her.

"How are you doing at school?" Mary looked at her for a second and replied, "I was first in class in the quarterly exams. But now..." her lips trembled and a slow tear ran down her cheeks, "Now, I am losing so many classes... Don't know if I will write my exams."

---

3 *Beti* - Daughter

"Did they both quarrel?"

Mary did not reply for a long time. Just when Olivia was about to leave, Mary turned and laid her head on her shoulders. Through the few words that escaped between her sobs, Olivia learnt that Aaron had brought another woman to live in their house and after a showdown, Sophie had left home.

Olivia never questioned Sophie or Mary again. She put Mary in a local school and life went on. Slowly, Sophie began showing interest in life. She started helping Olivia in running the estate. Sophie found her fun-loving self again. Mary was also doing well in school and Olivia began to feel that it was good that Aaron and Sophia had separated.

❁❁❁

It was a year since Sophie had come back. One day, a car drew up outside the bungalow and Olivia was worried when she saw Aaron step out. She wished Sophie would be steadfast and not be taken in by his false promises.

But she was aghast when Sophie announced that Mary and she were going home with Aaron. Olivia tried warning Sophie against such a move but her daughter stoically defended Aaron and insisted he had turned a new leaf.

Olivia shouted and argued with Sophie but could not change her mind. As a last resort, she threatened to not take back Sophie or Mary back in case something went wrong. Except that her shoulders squared and her lips turned up in determination, there was no change in Sophie's decision.

That was the last Olivia saw of her daughter. Within a month, she got the news that Sophie had killed herself. Mad with grief and guilt, Olivia died a hundred deaths. With the help of Pauline and Michael, she found that Aaron had begun beating Sophie again and rather than coming back to Ooty, she had taken her own life. She also tried her best to bring Mary to live with her but Aaron refused.

Except for taking down Sophie's and Aaron's wedding photo from the wall and breaking it into a million pieces with a hammer, there was nothing much Olivia could do.

❋❋❋

More than 10 years had passed since Sophie's death. Olivia had not been keeping well. There were times when she felt so tired that it called for great will power just to get up from the bed. Giving in to Pauline, she went for a check up. The doctors hemmed and hawed and finally told her that she had a terminal illness. She would live for only another six months.

After two days of self pity and tears, Olivia sat down to deal with death or rather her life until death. She called Pauline and Michael over to Ooty and asked them if they would like to run the estate. When they declined, she put up the estate for sale and left the negotiations and paperwork to Santhosh, her manager.

She called over her lawyer Seetharaman and discussed her final will with him.

Everything was ready within a month and Olivia called for a family meeting at Silver Oaks. She had not wanted to invite Aaron but Pauline and Michael insisted. They spoke to her about forgiving and family till she was sick of it. Olivia had lived with her anger too long. Only after much persuasion from Pauline and Michael, did she agree to name Aaron in the will.

This morning, when the will was read out, Aaron was angry.

"Just 10 Lakhs? 10 petty Lakhs for the son-in-law and 25 lakhs for the housekeepers? You need not have called me for this. I think the whole purpose was to insult me".

"Ten lakhs for a murderer. That's how I think about it. You killed my daughter".

Olivia ignored the warning glances Pauline and Michael gave her.

"So you called me just to enrage me? If anything, you should be ashamed of yourself. Mary told me that you warned Sophie that you will never take her back. That is the reason my poor Sophie took her own life. Imagine a mother telling her daughter this."

"How dare you come and sit in my judgment! It is like the Satan giving a sermon".

"You are calling me Satan? Let me tell you plainly what I think about you. You are a daughter killer. You are incapable of loving anyone in the world. You are just money making machine with absolutely no motherly feelings… You are..."

"Stop this very minute! You have come to receive alms from me shamelessly and you have the audacity to call me names? I am not giving you anything. I am going to remove you from the will and I will do it this very night before anyone tries to change my mind."

Olivia stalked out and shut herself in her room. Pauline entreated her to open the door and behave decently. Sarala and Menon pestered her to eat something. She ignored everyone.

❖❖❖

Olivia heard the grandfather clock in the hall strike 12. Despite the fire and the closed window, she shivered. She felt that something was going to go wrong.

The silence of the night was broken by a knock on her door.

She asked irritably, "Who is it?"

"Aaron".

She hesitated for a minute and then steeling herself for a confrontation, she limped to the door and opened it.

"Yes. What do you want? How much ever you grovel before me, I am not going to change my mind. I am removing you from the will".

Aaron looked confused.

"But... but didn't you send me the note asking me to meet you alone at midnight?"

"I asked you to meet me? I don't want to lay my eyes on you my whole life. Say whatever you want and get out. Don't give me lame reasons for your visit".

Still confused, he said, "Look. I have no interest in talking to you. But this note was in my room. It says,

"Come to my room alone at exactly midnight. Don't tell anyone. We can reach a compromise. ODM"

Olivia reached out and snatched the note. "I never sent it. I don't intend to compromise. I am planning to cut you out of my will and I will definitely do it". She tore the note into small pieces and threw them into the fire.

"You old hag! Who do you think you are! I will fight the will in the court and get every rupee due to me. My daughter has rights to the money".

Olivia's voice rose up in anger. "First thing you deceive my daughter and marry her for her money. Then when u knew you were not getting anything more, you kill her and now you are talking about your daughter's rights. I will use my money and prove in the court that Mary was not even born to you".

Aaron lost all his cool and began shouting," Are you crazy? You hag, I will kill you with my bare hands for what you just said. You are going to die by my hands..." he tried to strangle her.

Hearing the commotion, Menon and Sarala came running and Menon got Aaron off Olivia with difficulty. By then, there were sounds of people opening doors, shouting and running down stairs.

Olivia spoke to Menon in a hoarse whisper, "I don't want to talk about this to anyone. You explain to them what happened but don't let anyone knock on my door. I want to rest".

As she closed the door firmly, she could see Menon and Sarala talking to Pauline, Michael and Mark.

***

Inspector Palanivel sipped his first cup of tea for the day and opened the newspapers. Aged around 40, he had dark curly hair just graying at the temples and was lean and fit. Constable Murugan entered and removed his coat, still shivering. The phone rang shrilly, shattering the quiet of the morning.

"Ooty police station," Palanivel answered the phone. "I will be there in 15 minutes," he ended the call and walked out, leaving his cup of tea unfinished.

As he put on his coat, he barked at Murugan, "Murder at Silver Oaks. Call forensics and fingerprints". As he neared the door, he paused and said, "Call Detective Raj and ask him to join me there.

As he parked the jeep at Silver Oaks and stepped out, Palanivel saw Raj parking his bike. Raj was close to his age, about 5.7 feet tall and with dark brown intelligent eyes.

They entered the house and were shown into a big hall by Menon. Pauline was hunched up on the sofa, crying quietly. Sarala was serving tea and everyone was refusing. Aaron was lounging about, defiance written all over him.

Suddenly, they heard a car screech to a halt outside and saw a poised young woman enter the house. Her eyes searched around the room and finally settled on Aaron. She moved towards him with an easy grace and calling him "Papa", laid her hands on his.

***

Palanivel and Raj were seated in the sitting room. Both of them were comfortable working together. Usually,

Palanivel did the questioning and Raj just observed. They would later put the case together with their own insights. They had cracked many cases together.

First, a constable entered and briefed them about the murder. Next, Doctor Vincent came in to sit by them, cleared his throat and said, "She has died by a single bullet shot through her heart. She has been shot at from at least a distance of 10 meters. So suicide is ruled out. Going by the rigor mortis I guess she must have died any time between 11 pm and 2 am. More after the autopsy."

After the doctor left, a constable hurried in carrying a revolver held by a handkerchief. "I found this in the bushes in the garden, sir. The fingerprints people checked. It's wiped clean".

After instructing the constable about storing the revolver safely, Palanivel turned towards Raj and said, "Looks like a straightforward case. Menon went and stopped Aaron in the nick of time. Aaron then goes into the garden and keeps on obsessing about the altercation. Then gets very angry and rushes to the window and shoots her. Drops the gun into the bushes after wiping the fingerprints and goes up back to his room and waits for the body to be discovered".

"Where did he get the gun from?" Raj pondered.

"Open secret. Olivia had it lying in a drawer in the hall. She had bought it a few years back when there was a scare about burglars."

Raj smiled at him and said, "According to what we hear, Aaron decided to kill Olivia on the spur of the moment. But taking the gun out, shooting her, wiping the fingerprints off it... it sounds so planned".

"Raj, you never like a straightforward case. You always like to complicate it".

Menon was the first to be interviewed. He came in, took the towel lying on his shoulders and kept it on his arms, as a show of respect.

"Menon, I know how much you were attached to Olivia and how well you and Sarala took care of their family. Now we need you to tell us a few things so we can find out who killed her. Because this is a murder, you have to be frank and truthful," Palanivel explained and Raj just observed Menon from afar.

"Who discovered the body?"

"Sir, I did. She did not have any dinner yesterday. So I thought she may be hungry and went in to ask if I should bring in some tea."

"What time was it?"

"It was 6 AM. The time she normally wakes up. When I opened the door, she was lying in a pool of blood. I checked for pulse but she was dead".

Menon sobbed into his towel. Raj got up and put a hand on his shoulders and Menon calmed down.

Palanivel went on, "Where was the body lying? On the bed or out of it?"

"It was near the window".

"Was the window open or closed?" Raj asked.

"It was open, I think".

"Tell us all that happened yesterday".

Menon explained about the will being read out by Seetharaman and how Aaron got angry with Olivia. He also spoke about how she had shut herself in her room and how, later that night, he heard them shouting and had to pry Aaron off Olivia.

"What time did this happen?"

"Some time around 12.30. We were just going to bed".

"Where did Aaron go after that?"

"He went into the garden and then I went to bed. So I don't know what he did after that".

"Who locked up later then?"

"I think Aaron must have. Normally, we don't bother much about locking up at night because we have Roger and Rover. They are very fierce and don't let anyone in".

Raj and Palanivel exchanged a quick glance and Palanivel asked, "Did they bark at all last night?"

"No sir. They are not here anymore. Because madam sold Silver Oaks, she gave them away to a friend in the neighboring estate. In fact, only last morning did I take Roger and Rover to their new home".

Again, a quick exchange of glances and Palanivel asked, "Who decided they should be given away yesterday itself?"

"It was Olivia madam herself who asked me to take them away".

"Menon, normally is the window in madam's room open or closed?"

"Just before sleeping, madam definitely closed it daily. But some days, she liked to look out of the window before going to bed."

"Do you remember if they were open or closed when you went in to save madam from Aaron?"

"I am not very sure, but I think it was closed".

"What about the gun with which she was shot? Did you see it?"

"Yes. I saw it in the policeman's hand some time back. There was a gun in the house, lying in a drawer in the hall. It did look like the same one. I went and checked after that. It was not there where it usually lay".

"When did you last see it?"

Menon hesitated for some time, "Sir, to be frank, I don't even know when I saw it last. Madam bought it when there was a burglary scare in the neighborhood... some 4-5 years back. We used to be fascinated by it then. Cleaned it regularly. But after some time, everyone forgot about it".

"What about the ammunition?"

"I don't know. I think Madam had it in her own room".

"Can you think of anyone having an enmity with madam... maybe someone she was angry with or some estate worker she had fired or anything else?"

"No... Except Aaron there was no one she had a quarrel with. Wait… there is Shobana madam of the neighboring estate. She wanted to buy Silver Oaks but Olivia madam did not agree to the price which Shobana madam quoted. So finally, when Olivia madam sold the estate to someone else, Shobana madam came and quarreled with her".

"When did this happen?"

"Last week".

"That's all Menon; you can go and send Sarala in".

There was a sound of a throat being cleared. "Wait", spoke Raj for the first time. His voice was strong and resonant. "In the last two days, did you feel anything was strange or somehow different?"

Menon looked up and hesitated. "Yes... but it has no relation to the murder. I was just puzzled by something that happened. Madam had a secretary called Santhosh. Madam got him a job in Coimbatore and let him go join immediately. Santhosh himself offered to wait till the will was read and all estate matters settled but madam forced him to go.

Madam is usually very strict. She had asked me to find a job too but she had strictly told me that I can go only after she left Ooty. Please don't think I am being unkind to her. She has named me in the will and I am very thankful to her. I planned to be with her and serve her till she needed me. But since you asked if there was anything different, I was reminded of how madam forced Santhosh to go immediately and how it was out of character".

"Ok Menon, you can leave now", said Palanivel and after he left, Raj spoke from behind, "This case seems to be becoming more puzzling. If Aaron is the murderer, then there was no need to get the dogs away as they would not have barked at him. But the dogs have been moved. But does that tell us who the murderer is? No! It was the victim who got the dogs away!"

"Maybe, it was just a coincidence?"

"Exactly on the day a murder is committed, both the dogs leave the estate. How can that be a coincidence?"

Sarala knocked on the door and entered. She was middle-aged with a quiet efficiency about her. She confirmed that it was around 12.30 am when they went into Olivia's room and found Aaron trying to strangle her.

Raj asked her about the window and she confirmed that it was shut in the night but open in the morning when the body was discovered.

"Menon said the lady from the neighboring estate, Shobana, quarreled with Olivia. Were you there when it happened?" Palanivel asked.

"Yes. Shobana madam was angry with Olivia madam because she sold the estate to a stranger. Shobana madam's estate is next to ours and to go to their bungalow they need to go through our gardens. She was worried that the new owners may not agree to it".

"What did Madam say?"

"Madam also was angry with her and finally, Shobana madam shouted that she would kill Olivia madam before the sale. Ohhh..."

Palanivel caught her eye. "Yes. It is possible she may have killed her. Do you think she did it?"

"Don't know, sir. When she said that, we never thought she was serious. But now I don't know what to make of it. But everyone thinks it is Aaron who killed her".

"We are still checking. What are your plans next?"

"We will be going back to Palakkad. There was a tea shop up for sale and we didn't have money to buy before. But now that madam has left some money for us in her will, we will be able to buy it and settle down there."

Raj addressed Sarala for the first time, "Did you feel anything different in Olivia madam's behavior in the last few days?"

Sarala turned around to see Raj. She hesitated and then continued, "Very strange that you asked. I felt that madam somehow knew she was going to die".

"Not only Olivia, but everyone knew she was going to die in six months".

"Not that. Let me explain. Yesterday, it was around 5 am when I had just woken up and was going through the hall to the kitchen. I saw that madam was standing by the window, looking out to the estate. When she saw me, she asked me to bring her some tea made from tea leaves from our own estate. When I brought it to her, she took the cup from me and remarked that it will be the last cup she ever has. I saw tears in her eyes. When I hesitated, not knowing what to do, she told me to hurry as the will reading was to begin soon. And it turned out to be true. That was the last cup she drank".

"Okay, you can leave now. If I need anything more, I will call you".

Palanivel was silent for a while. After making sure Sarala left the room, he asked Raj, "Do we believe this? Maybe she is making it up. Or maybe she was being blackmailed and knew he was going to kill her".

"There was a ring of truth in what she said, but I definitely don't believe in premonitions".

"Okay, but why do you keep asking everyone about the window?"

Raj smiled and replied, "Think. The window was closed during the Aaron incident. But Olivia was killed by a shot from the open window. So someone or Olivia herself must have opened the window some time. Why would she open it after she had retired for the night?"

"Aaron must have come from the garden and knocked or called her from outside to open"

"I am keeping my mind open about who the murderer is..." Raj's voice trailed as they watched Aaron walk in with a swagger.

"Inspector, I did not commit the murder, though I wish I had done it. The old cat was instigating me into doing it". Neither Palanivel nor Raj answered.

Aaron went on, "After the will reading fiasco, she went into her room and shut herself in. My sister-in-law and the housekeepers kept trying to make her come out but she refused".

Still, no reaction from both.

"I know you may not believe what I am going to say. But it is the full truth. After dinner, I went into my room and found a note pushed under my door. It said 'Come to my room alone at exactly midnight. Don't tell anyone. We can reach a compromise. ODM."

"Where is that note?"

"Hmmm... I think she threw it into the fireplace when she got angry with me".

"So convenient... you don't have it. Now we have only your word that there was a note".

"Inspector, if I wanted to kill her, I would have done a better job. I went in and had that famous quarrel with her. When she said she could prove my Mary was not my daughter, I lost my cool, flew into a rage and tried to strangle her. After Menon pulled her away from me, I went to the garden and smoked for a while and later went back to my room".

"Did you know Olivia had a gun?"

"Yes. Everyone knew about it. She kept it in a drawer near the dining table".

"Did you take it out yesterday?"

"No. I didn't even think of the damned thing till everyone in the morning spoke about her being shot by it".

"How are your finances? Would the money from Olivia have helped you?"

His reply was marked by hesitation, "I think I'd better be frank with you. My finances are in very bad shape.

My investments had gone pretty bad recently. That is why I came down from Chennai when the old hag...sorry... Olivia asked me to come. I thought she had relented at last and would be giving me a sizable amount and I could let my Mary go abroad to study".

"So, why were you upset with the amount she offered?"

Aaron was filled with spite when he said, "This estate is worth around 10 crores. So by right, I or at least my daughter deserve five crores. And that old hag gives me a paltry 10 Lakhs. Imagine! Even Menon and his wife were getting 25 Lakhs. I am sure she kept the amount so low just to insult me".

"So how much is required for your daughter to study abroad?"

"At least 15 Lakhs."

"Okay. You can leave now. Please don't leave the town".

Finally to Raj's question of finding anything strange recently, Aaron thought for a while and said "No".

But he changed his answer before he left, "You asked me if I felt something was strange. I kept feeling that Olivia was trying to instigate me. Not just at night but also during the will reading, her attitude was as if she wanted me to be mad at her. I mean, I know she was cut up when Sophie killed herself. But this was not that. There was a look in her eyes... as if...as if she was watching me and was happy when I got angry with her".

"Come on Raj, what are your instincts? Do you still believe Aaron did not kill her?"

Raj snapped, "Tell me Palani, why do you think Aaron killed her? Trying to strangle her was because Olivia suggested that Mary was not his daughter. That is enough reason for him to get really mad. But she was saved. According to you, later, as he smoked, he must have planned the murder. So what must have been the reason for it?"

"Money. He didn't want Olivia to change the will. He didn't want to be done out of the 10 Lakhs. So he remembered the gun and brought it out, went back to the garden and knocked on the window. Then he shot her when she opened it and wiped the gun clean, dropped it into the bushes and went back to his room, cool as a cucumber. He pretended to be surprised in the morning when the murder came to light".

Raj shook his head as if he was not convinced.

"What about that note? I am sure he is lying".

"Hmmm…maybe someone is interested in getting Aaron hanged. They must have written it so that he was present in Olivia's room at the time the murder was committed".

"But the murder was committed later".

"Maybe something went wrong and the murderer had to postpone it".

The door opened again and Mary came in. She came in gracefully and sat down in front of Palanivel. Looking at her, he thought to himself, "This one is a cool customer.

Given a chance, I won't be surprised if she were a party to the murder. May be she is the planner and Aaron just executed it".

She looked directly into his eyes and said without any preamble, "My dad didn't kill her, Inspector".

"If it was not your dad, then who killed her?"

"Inspector, you are barking up the wrong tree. Let me explain. When you look for a murderer, you need to check for three things. Whether someone has a motive, whether he is at the scene and whether he has an alibi. There is a person in the house whom you have neglected all the time who fits these to a T".

Palanivel was taken aback.

"Mark. My esteemed cousin. He was very much on the premises. He has his own bedroom, so he will not have an alibi. And motive? Mark not only smokes and drinks, he is into drugs. His parents came to know about it and had him put into a rehab centre. Once he was out, they were worried about keeping him in Chennai. They were afraid his friends there would pull him back into it again. So they sent him to Ooty to be with grandma".

"How do you know all this?"

"In Chennai, we move in the same circles although Mark pretends he doesn't know me".

"Ok, then?"

"Two days ago, grandma caught him smoking a joint and had threatened to tell his parents. He was to go back to Chennai if he kept away from drugs. But she caught him at it and told him she was going to tell his parents that he should be in Ooty for another year at least. I heard she yelled her head off at him and that too in front of the servants. He retorted that he was very happy that she was sick and was going to die. Thinking like a typical addict, he considers anybody stopping him from doing drugs, is enemy".

"How do you know this? You were supposed to be in Chennai?"

"My dad heard the whole thing and called to tell me. I have always hated Mark and dad knew I would be thrilled by this bit of news".

"Is that reason enough to kill her?"

"You never know with these druggies. Maybe he didn't really plan it. But when he saw the possibility of my dad being blamed for the murder, I am sure he must have used it. After my dad went to bed, he could easily have gone to the hall, taken the gun out, knocked at her window and shot her when she opened it".

"Have you ever come to Ooty after you left with your mom all those years ago?" Raj broke the silence.

She turned around to look at him. "No. Olivia asked me to come back after my mom died. I had a weak spot for the old girl. She had treated me quite well when I was here with mom but I felt dad needed me more. So I refused and she was so angry with me then. But much later, maybe two years ago, she called me and after that, we have chatted once in a while on the phone. But I have never visited her".

She wiped a tear before continuing, "I think I am becoming a sentimental fool. But I really wish I had come to Ooty and visited her. I should have come along with dad and been nice to her. Who knows! She might even have funded my MBA abroad," she finished.

Not receiving a reaction, she got up and left.

"What do you make of her?" asked Palanivel.

"I think she is a worried young person beneath all that show of confidence. She is mighty worried that her dad may get arrested and was hell bent on putting us off course," Raj surmised.

"So you think all that news about Mark was a lie?"

"Definitely not. I don't think Mary is a fool. I am sure she knew we could ask and find out soon enough. But I feel she used the incident just to direct or rather misdirect our attention towards the wrong person."

***

Pauline came in and sat down. Her eyes were red and swollen.

To put her at ease, Palanivel summarized for her. "So, during the will reading, Olivia and Aaron had a quarrel and she went in and shut her door and never came out ... not even for dinner. Later, Aaron went in around midnight and quarreled with her again and tried to strangle her. But Menon and Sarala stopped him. Correct?"

"Yes, correct. Wait... when you summarized, I remembered something.. *Mama*[4] had come out of her room once, when we were having dinner".

"What?"

---

4 *Mama* - Mother

"Yes. What with the murder and all that followed, I had forgotten completely about it. We were having dinner and Menon and Sarala were serving us. Normally, from where we sit, we cannot see the corridor. But while eating, my fork fell and I bent down to pick it up. That's when I saw her crossing the corridor".

"Did you see her go back into her room?"

"No. I didn't keep a lookout as such. But she must have gone back and I could not have noticed. Like I told you, that corridor is not visible from the dining room".

"You said she crossed the corridor... what is there on that side?"

"There is the kitchen on the right side, from where she came. On the other side, there is a guest room, and next to it, there is a door which opens into the garden".

"Would the garden door have been open then?"

"Yes. As the bungalow has so many doors, we are not that particular about closing them all the time. Just before going to bed, Menon closes them all. As we have Roger and Rover around, we do neglect such precautions".

"But that day, they were not around?"

"Yes. I had forgotten. *Mama* had given them away to a friend. Yes. Menon had taken them out on that very day".

"Could Olivia have come out to drink some water or look for some food?"

"Menon and Sarla always make sure that the fridge in Olivia's room is stocked with water. Anyway, I saw her go past the kitchen, not towards it".

"What time did this happen?"

"Let me think… we started dinner a little late because of the will-reading fiasco. No one was in a mood. It must have been about 9".

Raj called out from his chair, "Just give me an idea of the sleeping arrangements".

"*Mama* had one of the bedrooms on the ground floor. There is an outhouse behind the kitchen where Menon and Sarala live. The outhouse is away from the bungalow and can be reached from the kitchen by a pathway. Then next to the dining area, there is a bedroom which used to be Sophie's bedroom... Aaron was put up in this room. Upstairs, Michael and I use the master bedroom which *Mama* had earlier. There are two more bedrooms upstairs. One is where Mark always sleeps. The other one is used only when there are guests".

"Describe what happened after the will reading and Olivia left the room angrily".

"I ran behind her and pleaded with her to let Aaron have the money. But she just brushed me aside and went into her room. When I came back, Michael was pacifying Aaron and telling him to try talking to her the next day before she changed the will. Later on, I went in and tried asking *mama* to have some food. She refused. Later at night, we all had dinner and went to sleep early. When we heard the commotion, we came out of our room and noticed that Mark too was coming down to check. After we heard about the incident, we discussed for a while and Michael and I left".

"What about Mark? Did he also go to his room?"

"No. He said he was not very sleepy and would watch TV in the hall and go to sleep later".

"Do you know when he finally came up to his room?"

"No. We slept immediately".

"Okay, you can go. If you remember anything connected with the case, you can come back and tell us."

After the door closed behind her, Palanivel said excitedly, "You know what? I think Olivia was being blackmailed. I had a suspicion before but now I am sure. It can explain everything. I think she went to meet him in the garden when the family was at dinner".

"And?" Raj asked.

"I think he asked her for some money and she refused. Then he waited till everyone went to sleep and then killed her".

"With the gun which was inside the house? Anyway, blackmailers never kill their victims. Victims are the geese which lay the golden egg. What secret could Olivia have for which she could have been blackmailed?"

"Maybe she knew something about her neighbors. Or maybe she herself was a blackmailer and one of her victims killed her".

"Where do you get such melodramatic ideas from? Most of the time, the reason for murders is simple and straightforward. Let's get on with the job".

The next person to enter the room was Michael. He was around 45 years old, clean shaven and had a 'happy go lucky' vibe about him. Today, however, he looked tired and a little worn.

"Hello. I am Michael and I work for a software company in Chennai. I am married to Pauline, Olivia's first daughter. I have a son who is doing his MBA. Since I am, or rather, my wife is going to inherit the entire estate, I am your prime suspect," he said disarmingly.

Either he is innocent or a wonderful actor thought Raj to himself and settled down to observe him, while Palanivel interviewed him.

"Since you are the one who is not directly affected by the tragedy, we can be frank with each other. So, first thing, what are your impressions? Do you think Aaron killed her?"

Michael took some time to think and answered carefully, "Personality wise, Aaron is capable of doing it. He is ruthless, has no great love for Olivia and is in great need of money. But whether he really did it or not I cannot say… because there is a contradiction".

"How?"

"There were two murder attempts. The first one was when he tried strangling her. That was a result of his sudden anger when she instigated him. But then she was saved. This sits very well with his personality. But, next, he is supposed to have gone to the garden, smoked for some time and then shot her deliberately, after a lot of planning, so he is not done out of the 10 Lakhs. This is not like him".

"You think that he could not have done it for such a small amount?"

Michael hesitated for some time. It looked as if he was debating with himself. Then he continued "I am not very happy that I am sharing this with you. It somehow feels like I am betraying the family. But I think I'd better tell you the truth or anyway you will learn about it soon. Aaron has gambling debts and the mafia is after his life. So 10 Lakhs is a good amount to put them off. Also, he has promised to come clean with Mary. So if his debts are cleared, he has more chances of leading a normal life hereafter. What I meant when I said it was against his personality was that he is a man of instincts and not of planning. I don't think he is the murderer as the second attempt required much planning".

"What about your son? We heard he too has been having some problems with Olivia?"

Guilt crossed Michael's face but he managed to cover it with a sheepish smile. "Now who has been carrying tales to you? Yes. Like I came clean about Aaron, I should have told you about it. But you know how it is. When it is your own flesh and blood, you tend to overlook".

As if he was deciding how much to say, he let out a long sigh and began talking fast as if to cover up his embarrassment. "Mark has been a problem child. In college, he got into drugs and had to be admitted into a rehab centre. And yes, we had sent him to Olivia so that he would not relapse. Olivia caught him smoking a joint and scolded him. That's all".

"One of our sources said Mark could have killed Olivia".

Hearing Raj's statement, Michael's demeanor changed. His confidence fell way and his shoulder sagged. He leaned back in his chair and closed his eyes.

"You know, Inspector, I have been worried to death about this possibility. After we saved Olivia from Aaron, Pauline and I went back to our room. In the morning, when we found Olivia dead, I mentally checked where we had seen Mark last. I remember seeing him looking out of the hall window. Pauline asked him to come up and he said he wanted to watch some TV. I have absolutely no idea when he went to bed. I don't know whether he shot her".

Once he spoke his heart out, all energy seemed to leave him. "Inspector, please go ahead and check the possibility about Mark. But if you find evidence that he has, indeed, killed her, then please let me know first as I want to prepare Pauline for the shock. She has no idea that I suspect Mark".

Michael left the room with heavy steps, a shadow of the suave man who had entered the room some 10 minutes ago.

***

The last person to be interviewed, Mark shuffled in with unfocused eyes and at least a week-old beard.

He settled himself in front of Palanivel, but kept fidgeting. Palanivel used his 'tough-cop' voice and asked, "When did you go to sleep last night?"

Mark remained silent and Palanivel was thinking if he should repeat the question, when suddenly he leaned forward and said, “I helped *pa* drag Aaron Uncle away from grandma. Then I went directly to my room and slept”.

“But someone said they saw you in the hall, watching TV, after the Aaron fiasco was done”.

“Maybe I was around for some time. I don’t remember,” Mark kept scratching his chin through his beard.

“Do you think Aaron killed her?”

He suddenly flared up in anger. “It is your duty, as police, to find out. Why are you asking me? I am not the police here”.

Realizing he had to mind his manners, he calmed down, “I mean, it was so confusing, with so many things happening around, I just don’t remember”.

“If not Aaron, who do you think could have killed her?” Raj asked.

With great difficulty, Mark changed his focus from Palanivel to Raj. Palanivel could actually see his pupils dilating and then constricting as he found the source of the voice.

He seemed to rack his brains, as he concentrated on finding an answer. Then suddenly, he exclaimed, “I know who killed her!”

His elation at finding the answer was suddenly replaced by a sly look. “It was last week... the old cat... I am sorry, she is dead... so I should respect her, shouldn't I? Ok... gran didn't know I was around. But I was smoking, sitting under the library window and she and that secretary of hers, Santosh, were talking in whispers. When their conversation became heated, they raised their voices. Gran was arguing about some money withdrawals".

"How much was the amount? And why was Olivia refusing to give it?"

Again Mark consciously concentrated on his answer, "Am not very sure but it was a very big amount. I couldn't hear them properly. Just that they discussed some really huge amount." He grinned foolishly and said, "I remember thinking I could buy so much of... I mean... what I meant is I could buy... Hmmm.. I could buy some books," he finished lamely.

"Think well. This may give us a good idea about who could have killed her".

Mark screwed up his face and rubbed his eyes and thought but didn't seem to remember any more about the incident.

Palanivel spoke hesitantly, as if worried about Mark's reaction, "Did you kill her?"

Whatever reaction he expected, he was not prepared for what happened. Mark began sobbing uncontrollably, "I did not... I did not... I hated her, true. She scolded me so much in front of the servants and treated me as if I were a kid. Then I wanted to strangle her there itself but I didn't have the guts. I was always a scaredy cat. That was how my cousin Mary taunted me when I was a kid...

I hate her for that but she is right... I never had guts..." the outpour seemed to exhaust him.

Palanivel did not know what to do with him. He simply asked Mark to leave.

As soon as the door was shut, Palanivel turned towards Raj and spoke. "See, sir, my guess about a blackmailer seems to be right. I think it was Santosh who was blackmailing her. Once the money was transferred into his account, he left Ooty and then he must have realized she may report him to the police. So he must have just come back and killed her that night".

Raj appeared to be thinking deeply. He replied hesitantly, "Hmmm...Though circumstances seem to point to what you are saying, I am not convinced. There are too many things... like it was too big a coincidence that the very night when Olivia read the will, the very night when Aaron tried to kill her, Santosh too came up to Ooty and could borrow the gun from the hall and shoot her without anyone seeing him. Anyway, I am not very convinced with what our friend told us just now. His drug-crazed brain may not have understood what Olivia and Santosh discussed but I do agree we need to talk soon to this Santosh".

Palanivel seemed to be on his own trail of thought. "Did you notice how he behaved? I am sure he must have taken some drugs just before coming in. His nose was watery, his eyes bloodshot, he kept having highs and lows and got angry and cried for no reason".

Raj smiled at him mischievously and said, "As usual, you have read the symptoms correct but your diagnosis is wrong. Those were not signs of drug intake but withdrawal symptoms".

Palanivel looked crestfallen, but went on, "We have finished with all. Do you want to question someone again?"

"Call Michael back".

A very subdued and dull Michael came in. Raj asked him, "Do you have access to Olivia's accounts? Can you find out if there has been any huge withdrawal from the account recently?"

Michael was guarded when he replied, "I don't think so. I mean I can't find out about it. Olivia was very secretive about her finances all through. After the sale of the estate, she closed the estate account and deposited all the sale proceeds into a new account with a new bank. She showed me the new passbook and the credit of the sales proceeds into it. She also gave me the new Cheque books etc."

***

Constable Murugan was on the phone.

Palanivel was telling Raj the story of Olivia's daughter Sophie and her suicide.

Murugan kept the phone in its hook and turned towards Palanivel, "No one seems to know where this Santosh is working now. At the estate, everyone vaguely said he got a job in Coimbatore. But no office address… no contact address... no information".

"Raj sir, here is more proof that Santhosh must have killed her. He has informed everyone at the estate that he has a job in Coimbatore. Later, he came and killed her and then ran away to some unknown place with the blackmail money Olivia must have given him".

Raj shook his head and started pacing in the verandah attached to the front office. As he passed by, Palanivel remarked, "May be the neighbor Shobana did it?"

Raj paused mid-stride and gathered his thoughts, "You remember, each and every person had some information to give us. Like, Olivia being out of her room that night, and letting Santosh go away soon, the dogs being taken away… all these are bits of a huge jigsaw puzzle. Yes, I want to question Shobana also. But only for additional information and not because I suspect her. Somehow, I can't imagine her coming all the way in the middle of the night, getting the gun out of the house and standing under the window, expecting Olivia to open it and then kill her".

The phone started ringing shrilly. Palanivel picked the receiver.

"Ootacamund police station. Yes, Palanivel speaking. What! Are you sure? I can't believe this. Who had done it then? Oh ok… yes. Now my work is over. I will send you all the details".

He turned towards Raj, savoring the moment before breaking the suspense, "That was Chennai police. It seems there was an attempt to murder a politician yesterday, but they nabbed the guy. Under interrogation, he broke down and admitted that he was a hired assassin. Someone had paid him to kill the politician. When questioned further, he said he had murdered a rich old woman here in Ooty two days ago, also for a huge amount".

"Who gave him the money?"

"It seems he does not know. A sum of 25 Lakhs was transferred to his account and the instruction was that he would find a gun placed in a cover in the rose bushes. He was to take it, be on the spot, before the ground floor window. At about 1 am, a lady would be seen at the window. He was instructed to shoot her, wipe the gun, throw it back in the bushes and leave".

'Hmmm... So everything went according to plan?"

"Yes. He had gone back to Chennai and was on his next project when he got caught… unfortunately for him, but fortunately for us. The case is over for us now".

Raj quietly looked at him for a minute and said, "No. The case is not over. But it has become more interesting now".

"My God, I have been blind!" he exclaimed. He looked at Palanivel with a mysterious smile and said, "Come, Let's go to Silver Oaks estate. I now know who got Olivia murdered".

By the time Palanivel reached the jeep, Raj was already seated in it.

"It must be Santosh, that's why you did not want Murugan to bring the handcuffs. We will find him and bring him to Ooty. I guess it was blackmail. I knew it all along. Though I can't understand Olivia's secret."

"If not Santosh, then who else can it be? Is it Shobana? Yes it must be so. You said she could not have come all the way to the estate. But now it is this assassin. So she must have paid him?"

Raj's silence frustrated Palanivel.

***

All the people in the house had gathered in the library. Raj was like a live wire and kept pacing the room.

Michael asked with hesitation, "Have you caught the murderer? Do you know who killed Olivia? We heard it was not any of us but a hired person".

Raj stopped pacing and said, "Yes. It was a hired assassin but someone paid him a large amount to kill her. And I know who paid him".

"Then you can rule me out. I don't even have 100 rupees to pay anyone," said Aaron.

"Yes. You are clear. It is not you." said Raj.

"Then who had the money to pay the assassin?"

"Someone who had lots of money and was willing to spend for the murder".

Everyone followed Raj's movement.

"The person who transferred the amount and gave instructions about every step is none other than Olivia herself".

There were shouts of "It can't be", "I can't believe it", "Why did she do it" etc. Raj waited till the confusion died.

"The motive for the murder/suicide was revenge. She wanted to punish Aaron by putting him behind bars for a crime he did not commit, so that he would suffer for the crime he committed earlier. Olivia's guilt and inability to avenge Sophie's death had been preying on her. When she came to know about her imminent death, she went about plotting her sweet revenge. That's why she decided on such a small amount to be given to Aaron. He had rightly observed that every action of hers was directed at instigating him. She found an assassin and negotiated with him, all through emails. So he had no idea who she was. When Santosh questioned her about the huge transfer, she argued with him and Mark overheard them. She then found Santosh a job and moved him out before she could execute her plan. Then she closed the account and sold the estate and put all the money into a new account with a new bank. Then on the day of the will reading, she was up and having a last loving look at her estate, when Sarala found her in a sentimental mood. She also sent the dogs away so they would not bark when the assassin entered the estate. During the will reading, she kept instigating Aaron, so that he would quarrel with her. She waited till everyone was having dinner, then she scrawled that note to Aaron and pushed it under his door. That was when Pauline saw her from the dining table. She also took the loaded gun then, placed it in the rose bushes, and sneaked back. When Aaron came in at midnight, she again provoked him into trying to kill her. She also carefully tore up the letter and threw the pieces into the fire, so that he couldn't prove why he went to her room. Then she waited till 1 am and opened the window and coolly waited till she was shot by the assassin".

There was utter silence in the room as people took time to digest the words.

Mary went to Aaron and said "*Papa...*" and laid her head on his shoulders.

Raj turned towards her and said, "You, Mary... you were purposely redirecting our attention towards Mark, weren't you?"

"Yes. I was very worried that *papa* had done it. He is very short-tempered and in a fit of rage, he could have done it. I felt I had the duty to safeguard him".

"Lucky for him and you that the assassin was caught committing another crime and he confessed to this one too. Otherwise, it was a perfect crime. Inspector Palanivel would have arrested Aaron".

ROSIE..... ROSIE

The alarm went off, waking me from my deep slumber. I turned it off and sat on the bed for a few minutes, taking in the bleak contours of the room. I cursed that my house was near the railway station.

As a bachelor living alone, my sundry relatives arriving at the station expected me to receive them. "His house is just five minutes away. Just imagine, if not for the luggage, we can simply walk down."

As if that excused my having to put up with the trouble of waking up at 3 am to receive an old aunt who was coming by the Nethravathi Express. The train was slated to arrive at Coimbatore railway station at the unearthly hour of 3.30 AM!

Grumbling, I started my bike. The old lady better not have so much luggage that I will need to haggle with the notorious Coimbatore auto drivers.

As I turned down the road, the cool air of the early morning hit me. The dazzling full moon lit my way and made the city seem ethereal. What power the moon has! All the ugliness of a pulsing, growing city - the under-construction multi-storied structures sheathed beneath gaudy blue plastic, potholes and stones on the road, leaking sewer pipes, half-torn posters on overflowing garbage drums - all disappeared.

Instead, the moon shone on the road, laminating it silver, blinked off an orange light from a puddle of water, glinted golden off the leaves of a tree and made parallel black and silver patterns of wicker gates of houses on the half-lit roads.

❋❋❋

The railway station was deserted. "Who will be out on such a cold morning at this hour except suckers like me?" I thought to myself. As I reached the platform, I was engulfed by the heady smell of jasmine. Long strings of the flower lay coiled in baskets, shining white in the wee hours, probably waiting to be loaded onto a train. The sweet scent added magic to the hour. I lit a cigarette and waited. Suddenly, an announcement came on, loud and clear. The train was going to be an hour late.

Resigned to my fate, I decided to sit on the bench and wait. As I pulled on my cigarette contentedly, I observed an old man approaching and sitting beside me. He was dressed in a neat white *veshti*[5] and shirt. His eyes glinted through his specs. Then he cleared his voice and I knew my peace was going to be invaded.

"It's very cold, isn't it?" he attempted a conversation. I mumbled a reply and wished to god he wouldn't talk to me and let me snooze sitting there. Suddenly, there was a commotion on the opposite platform.

A shabby young man was yelling at the top of his voice. He had a dirty beard, his clothes were torn and there was a wild look about him. A few people in uniform were trying to pull him away. I realized he was repeating the

5 *Veshti* - Also known as dhoti, it is a rectangular piece of unstitched cloth wrapped around the waist by men

same word... crying in a heart-rending voice.. "Rosie... Rosie... Rosie..."

There was so much agony and grief in his voice that it affected me deeply and made me desperately sad for him. Finally, the attendants managed to pull him away, still shouting and crying in that sorrowful voice of his.

Long after he was gone, long after the platform returned to its silence, his voice kept echoing in my mind, reaching up to my soul.

"One small mistake can cost so much," the harsh voice of the old man interrupted me. With little encouragement from me, he began narrating the young man's story.

"Vallicchami *kounder*[6] was the richest man in a village near Pollachi; so rich and fierce that no one else in the village dared or wished to have the same name. So notorious for violence that people avoided him rather than anger him in any way. When his only son Avinash wanted to go to the US for higher studies, the *kounder* agreed even though he was not very happy about it. But it became a matter of pride because none of the village sons had gone there.

Vallichhami's main income was from growing groundnuts and coconuts and selling them to the oil mills. Also, he made easy profits on the sums he lent at a high interest to his business friends in Coimbatore city.

His heart would swell with pride when all his friends asked him about his son studying in 'Ammerikka'.

6 *Kounder* - A title used in parts of Tamil Nadu

So when the collector of Dharapuram proposed an alliance between his daughter Dhanalakshmi and the America son, Vallichhami was elated. He could finally achieve something that money could have never bought him - respect. The Dharapuram collector enjoyed a good standing in their community.

When Avinash informed he was coming for the holidays, Vallichami was determined to have the engagement before he returned.

But, Avinash brought Rosie with him.

Rosie… so beautiful but Anglo Indian… Dhanam was a *koundar*.

Rosie… so smart and intelligent but from a poor family… Dhanam was rich and cultured.

Rosie… so stylish and graceful but penniless... Dhanam had 100 acres of paddy to her name.

Father and son bickered constantly. None of their arguments convinced the other. Then, there was nothing more to be said. Finally, the *koundar* seemed to relent. He was amicable towards his son and Rosie and took them around the estates, giving them fresh *elani*[7] from their coconut trees, starting the motor pump and drenching them under the gushing water, driving them around on the tractor.

Then came the day for Avinash to leave and no engagement was celebrated. He was to go up to Chennai by train and take a flight from there. Vallichami accompanied them to the railway station.

7 *Elani* - Tender coconut water

The station was crowded as usual with passengers, people who had come to see them off, hawkers and porters. People milled around the train ticket examiner, hoping for a miracle and a berth.

There was a sudden buzz among the crowd as the train entered. Mothers were pulling their kids away from the tracks. Porters snapped out of their reverie. Passengers searched for their berths and came out to wave goodbye at the door after placing their luggage inside.

As the train was leaving, Avinash and Rosie were standing at the door of the AC 1st class compartment, waving to the family. The train was picking up speed.

Suddenly, all the pent up anger and frustration welled up in him and the *kounder* ran alongside, caught Rosie's hand, jerked her out and pushed her under the train - all in one swift move.

For a shocked moment, Avinash stared uncomprehendingly at his father. Then something snapped inside him. He jumped out of the train with a wail that was heard above the whistle of the train".

The old man stopped his narration abruptly and silence fell on the platform... His frigid storytelling had sent my imagination racing and completely immersed in it, I forgot my sleep.

By now, there was hardly a soul on the platform but us.

"And then?" I asked, leaning towards him.

Silent for a while, the old man cleared his throat and continued...

"Rosie died but Avinash was rescued and taken to the hospital. But a fate more cruel than death awaited him. He lost himself. Despite the care given by the mental institution, he would escape on some nights and visit the railway station, crying his heart out. Like he did today"

"What about the *koundar*?"

"Oh… he is alive. He managed to escape the police's clutches because of his wealth. He hardly talks to anyone and is morose and silent all the time. He roams around at odd hours. At least, the son has the luxury of lunacy. Very much sane, the father has recurring nightmares and is living a sleepless life of remorse and repentance".

A mobile phone shrilled, shattering the silence. I woke up from the spell cast by his story. I had forgotten where I was and why...still no sign of the train and no announcement. I stood up and stretched myself.

The old man was answering the phone, "Vallichami *kounda*r... Yes yes.... I know it is late. Ok Ok... I am coming home".

THE WEAPON

The African sun blazed down from the blue skies. I pushed the sunglasses firmly into place and waited for my driver, with the bags of fresh vegetables, fruits and groceries weighing heavily in my hands. Tesha, the well-built African, drove up and helped me with my bags.

As we drove home, I recalled how people had warned me about the insecure life in Africa - the thieving, the murders and slit throats. When I met Tesha for the first time, I had been very intimidated by his color and size. But in these three months, I realized that he was a giant genie and had become my ally. He struck bargains for me at the grocery, got the best rice from the market, took me to the hospital when I was unwell and helped me understand the African way of life.

But that did not allay all my fears. African strangers still scared me.

Before long, we reached the building.

"*Asante Sana*[8], Tesha" , I thanked him. Brushing aside his offer to help me with the bags, I got the door opened and stepped inside the house. My maid was absent for the day and I would have to do all the chores by myself,

8 *Asante sana* - Thank You in Swahili

starting with cleaning the kitchen and cutting the vegeta… "OH MY GOD!!!"

There were three of them. Their dark skin shone in the sunlight. They were huge and one of them had a long moustache. Preoccupied, they did not notice me. The automatic lock on the door had already fallen into place, blocking my escape from the house.

My heart was racing so fast I was worried they could hear it. Feeling weak at the knees, I edged my way carefully towards the sofa and sank into it.

Then I remembered the weapon.

But it was inside one of the bags. Without drawing attention to myself, I moved inch by inch and reached the bags.

Slowly… slowly…I felt for it....searched around.... and finally found it.

Triumphantly, I took it out and turning back, saw that one of them had paused. All three blindly rushed towards me. Fear coursing through me, I opened the Tik-20 and sprayed viciously at the three cockroaches.

KARMA

[7]Om Bhuur-Bhuvah Svah
Tat-Savitur-Varennyam |
Bhargo Devasya Dhiimahi
Dhiyo Yo Nah Pracodayaat ||

Hari *vadhyar* started his day early with his usual chant of *Gayatri Mantra*[9], without realising that the day was going to be anything but usual. After finishing it, he sat for a minute, thinking about the other Gayatri in his life. He always spoke to her in his mind, telling her about his feelings; sometimes joking with her and often chiding, as if she were really next to him.

Somehow the day seemed different. He felt a deep, unexplainable sadness in his heart. The ringing of the mobile phone pierced his thoughts.

"Hello?"

"*Vadhyar*[10], this is Srini. As per your instructions, I am going to Malkajgiri for the *Ayush homam*[11]. After the first birthday, I will proceed to Seethafal Mandi for the *grihapravesham*[12]..."

Hari *vadhyar*'s day had begun.

❖❖❖

9 *Gayatri Mantra* - a chant of the Vedic tradition

10 *Vadhyar* - a Tamil temple priest

11 *Aysuh Homan* - a ritual

12 *Grihapravesham* - Housewarming

Hari *Vadhyar* reached the small function hall on his motorcycle. He was officiating an engagement that day. A few of his younger assistants had reached the venue earlier and were ready with the initial rites.

The hall was filled with youngsters, all laughing and chatting. Everyone was in high spirits. Looked like the couple was from the IT sector. He sat down and started with the *mantras* that were to be chanted by the groom. But the young handsome guy was paying attention to his friends and clowning around.

Hari chanted the *mantra*[13] louder and taking cue, the groom repeated the words. Hari signed for the girl to be brought in and there was a flurry of activity and a hush descended over the gathering. The bride looked lovely in a blue silk *sari*[14].

Now the groom ignored his friends and talked to the girl, indifferent to the *mantras.* Hari paused till he had the attention of the couple and explained to the groom, "Please pay attention and also understand what the *mantras* mean. This is a social commitment on your side that you intend to marry this girl. Since I am the one chanting it and you are only repeating, it will appear like I am getting engaged. To avoid that, I will ask you to say *muma*[15] at certain points, which means mine. If you don't say muma, it will mean that I, Hari *vadhyar*, am getting betrothed to this girl and I intend to marry her and not you."

13 *Mantar* - chant

14 *Sari* - A length of cotton or silk draped around the body by women in parts of South Asia

15 *Muma* - an utterance during a ritual

The groom was confused. Hari explained further, "Sometimes, you have your secretary write letters for you. But it is not valid till you sign in the end. So your *muma* is the signature you give to make sure this is your engagement ceremony and not the *vadhyar*'s".

Laughter erupted from the crowd and the explanation had the groom and the bride paying total attention.

❁❁❁

Hari refused to eat at the function and came out to the parking lot. Now that his mind was not occupied, his heart was heavy again and he searched for a reason.

His phone rang. It was Iswaran *mama,* his friend.

"*Vadhyar*, I hope I am not disturbing you. I have a good friend, Raman, who has just arrived from the USA. He lost his wife in a car accident. He finished the cremation there but he wants to do the rites here. Can you do the *shraaddam* for him?"

Hari did not perform any rituals after the *shraddam*[16], as it was a rite for the dead. But since he did not have any other work for the day, he agreed and took the address.

❁❁❁

Hari rang the bell. The apartment was in a rich exclusive neighborhood. The teak door too spoke of opulence.

A middle-aged man, with despair in his eyes, opened the door. They spoke briefly, discussing what needed to be done. Hari followed him into the hall and sat down. It was then that he noticed the huge photo, framed and garlanded, on a side table.

---

16 *Shraddam* - a rite for the dead

He couldn't believe his eyes and kept staring at the photo. It couldn't be his Gayatri!

This was the reason for the sadness that shadowed him all day.

There was no doubt. It was his Gayatri! The same Gayatri, whom he still considered as wife.

He was shocked at first. Gayatri was dead? He could see from the photo that the years had added more beauty and maturity to her looks. His Gayatri, whose charming smile could light up the whole world, whose tinkling laughter was music, who would joke and wait with a naughty glitter in her eyes till he got it. Gayatri, who gave him all the love he ever received in his entire life.

Even though his lips chanted the *mantras*, his mind flew to his younger days.

❋❋❋

Having lost his parents at an early age, he was brought up by his uncle, Sunderasa Iyer, who was the *vadhyar* of Kalpathi, a village in Palakkad district of Kerala. Being a brilliant student, Hari had managed to get into an engineering college in Coimbatore. His uncle, loyal to his dead sister's son, paid the fees from his meager income.

But this made his aunt Lalitha resent him more. She ranted on about how the money being wasted on the orphan could make her two children's life more comfortable.

❋❋❋

Hari hated to ask for money. Worse still, today he had to ask his aunt. He hesitated and said "*Athai*[17], can I have 50 rupees? I need to renew my train pass."

Lalitha gave him a cold stare. Then she grudgingly gave him the money, murmuring to herself, "I have to cook and clean after him and I have to shell out hard-earned money. If only he could assist his uncle, then not only will my husband have less work, there will also be some more money in the house. But no! He thinks he is bigger than the *vadhyar* job. He wants to go to college and become an engineer".

Hari left with a heavy heart. Sometimes, he wished he could do what his aunt suggested; become a *vadhyar*. It was easy. He anyway knew most of the *mantras* and rituals but he loved to study. He found quantum mechanics fascinating. He wanted to know the intricacies of engineering. What other students found difficult to understand, he could grasp in a moment. It was this love for learning that helped him bear his aunt's and her friends' taunts.

❖❖❖

Hari stood behind the door of the moving train, looking at bluish violet hills fade into the distance. Like everyday, he wondered how his whole life changed once he was on the train. He was not the unloved, hated relative living off his uncle's money but a smart young student, envied and respected for his academic achievements. His faculty admired him for his intelligence and his classmates liked his simplicity and innocence.

---

17 *Athai* - Aunt in Tamil

He sensed someone come behind him and turned around, expecting one of his friends. But it was a young girl, slim and tall, with a ready smile on her face.

"Wow! The mountains are beautiful and the grass is so green." He stared at her, without trying to reply. He rarely talked to girls. And he had never known anyone so beautiful.

She continued, "In Hyderabad, there is not much greenery. Also, there are many rocks. By the way, I am Gayatri. We recently moved to Palakkad and I have joined an engineering college in Coimbatore".

After she left his side, he tried to remember everything about her. Her light pink *salwar kameez* [18] with a flowy *dupatta*[19] fluttering in the wind, her small earrings, the way her one tooth overlapped another and showed tantalizingly when she smiled. Above all, the fragrance that wafted from her.

When his friends teased him about the new girl who talked to him, Hari brushed it away with a smile but he kept thinking about her the whole day.

❖❖❖

Hari was sitting in the *thinnai*[20] and pouring over engineering graphics when he heard the neighbor's door being opened. He pinched himself when he saw Gayatri coming out.

---

18 *Salwar Kameez* - A type of Indian attire that consists of a long top and a pleated pant

19 *Dupatta* - Something similar to a shawl and is usually worn with a salwar kameez

20 *Thinnai* - Verandah in Tamil

"Hey! You are the one I saw on the train yesterday. Do you live here?"

He nodded, smiling happily.

"My dad is the manager of the Indian Overseas Bank branch in Kalpathi. He got transferred recently".

In Palakkad, girls did not speak to boys directly. Hari liked it a lot that Gayatri chatted with him easily. All his friends in college were envious of him and the easy friendship he shared with his lovely neighbor. She would often come looking for him with a pile of books, asking for his help in some subject or the other.

That was how their friendship began. Slowly, she began sharing her problems, her quarrels with friends, the gist of the stories she read, the songs she heard and the movies she watched.

❖❖❖

There was a song on his lips, a spring to his steps. He felt he was floating in air. He had never felt this happy in his entire life. He knew he was in love with Gayatri.

But wonder of wonders! She loved him too.

In her frank style, she told Hari that she enjoyed every moment of their time together; she could think of only her feelings for him and nothing else for the last few days. She told him that his sadness affected her deeply and she wanted to make him the happiest person… that she wanted to marry him and spend a lifetime together.

All the love that was amassed in his heart, because he had no one to give to, burst out and he was filled with the deepest feelings for her. Daily in the morning, with the sincerity of new-found faith, he thanked God for bringing Gayatri into his life.

❋❋❋

They were sitting on the rocks on the banks of the stream. It was their favorite meeting place.

He looked at her. A soft breeze that blew from the Western Ghats played with her hair. As she talked, she pulled a strand of hair that fell on her face and tucked it firmly behind her ear. He loved to see her do this.

"Hmmm..." said Gayatri, with a naughty glint in her eyes. "What shall I tell Mohan? He says in his love letter that he will die if I don't love him back!"

Hari replied, "But I will kill him if you say yes to him. So he is going to die anyway". Gayatri's laughter rang through his soul.

He took her hand in his and said, "Gayatri, I have never received love from anyone. I lost my parents when I was a few months old. Since then, it has been uncle and aunty. Despite aunty not liking the idea much, my uncle forced her to take me in. So you can imagine how she treats me. But you came into my life like spring in the desert. Now, I can't even think of life without you."

"Why should you think of a life without me? Now you are in your third year of engineering. In another year you will finish and get a job. After that, we will tell my parents and whether they agree or not, let us marry."

"But Gayatri, my aunt is very jealous of my happiness. She was telling uncle that you are always disturbing me and not letting me study. She who always gave me odd jobs during my exams and made me help with the kids' homework just before my practicals is now speaking about me not concentrating on studies!"

Gayathri looked upset. "You know Lalitha aunty has been gossiping about me. It seems a few of our neighbors told my mom that she has been spreading rumors about me; that I have a loose character and have several boyfriends. That I am trying to snare you, her precious nephew, because you are soon going to be an engineer and earn big money".

"Oh no! I didn't know that. Why is she grudging me my happiness? Gayatri, maybe you should stop coming over so often. I am worried that she will do something to you. You are very precious to me and I can't bear if something happens to you, my dearest."

❖❖❖

Hari was very low. He had not met Gayatri for a week. As colleges were closed for vacation, they could not meet on the train too. He kept looking out of the window to see if he could spot her.

Lalitha came into the room and glared at him. "Have you no gratitude towards us? All other time you have college or you are helping that slut from the next house. Now that you have holidays, can't you assist your uncle? He has gone out in the hot sun and has to walk back after eating a heavy meal at the *shraddam*. You could have taken the cycle and brought him back. No, your lordship is above all that. He has time only to stare at neighbor girls."

The comment about Gayatri stung him. He hated Lalitha with all his heart for daring to talk about his Gayatri. But he swallowed it and asked timidly, "Shall I go now?"

"No need. I know why you are offering. You just want an excuse to go out and look at the girls. I have cut a jackfruit from the tree and you can take all the flesh out. It will keep you busy for 3-4 hours. Meanwhile, I have to go help *modaks* in the temple. Every one in the house is not as lazy as you. We all need to work and bring in some money".

Hari sat down for the messy work with the fruit. As his hands worked, prying the flesh out, his mind raged. Then he heard the door opening and Gayatri entered furtively.

Having been starved of her sight since the last few days and wallowing in self pity, his eyes welled up with tears. She sat down next to him.

"It seems Lalitha aunty had come home and told my mom that while they were under the impression that I was at college, I was out with boyfriends, behaving like a slut. But my mom told her she trusted me and did not need advice from anyone about how to bring up her daughter".

"And?" he asked tensely.

"My mom has strictly instructed me against talking to you".

He gave her such a forlorn look that she placed a hand on his to reassure him.

"No, don't look at me like that. It doesn't change my feelings. Nothing in the world is going to change my decision. But in respect to my parents' wishes, maybe it is better we don't meet often."

Hari saw her slipping away from his life. Her assurances made him more insecure and the thought that she may never be his made him so miserable that his eyes reddened and a sob escaped him.

"Hari, stop it! I can't bear it if you are unhappy. Let us be wise now and think how we can continue our friendship without hurting my parents".

But Hari was inconsolable.

As his hands were sticky, he tried to wipe his tears on his shirt sleeves in vain. Gayatri moved next to him and lovingly wiped his tears. She leaned on his shoulders. It was a pure moment of 2 friends sharing their grief.

Suddenly, the door opened and Lalitha triumphantly entered with a few of her cronies. "I told you. Her mother said she was pure and innocent. Does this look so? I knew she will enter my house like a thief the moment I went out. That's why I waited at the end of the road to catch her. Saro... Go and call her mother. Let her come and see her precious daughter whom I have caught red-handed. What will her mother say now?"

❊❊❊

It was two days since Hari had eaten. Lalitha had first sent the kids to call him during meal times. Then she herself came, but he did not respond and now she had stopped asking him. He lay on the bed with his eyes closed. Everyone else had gone to sleep. His mind kept going back to the incident. He had asked his friend to find what happened to Gayatri.

The friend came back with the news that her parents had been devastated. Even though they had trusted her, they did not want to continue living in the village. They had taken their belongings and simply left.

Tears streamed down Hari's face. He felt that the heavens had opened for him just once and then closed for good. Now he was back in this hellhole. His mind refused to accept that he would never see his Gayatri again. Never hear her tinkling laughter, never match wit with her, never have anyone to share his deepest thoughts with. He had lost not just his girlfriend but a soul mate.

He sat up all of a sudden. He was not going to give her up so easily. He would go to Hyderabad and find her. He knew where his aunt kept the money. He got up noiselessly and stole the money. He would take a bus to Coimbatore and would somehow make it to Hyderabad.

***

Hari was tired and lost. He had come to Hyderabad with the belief that he could easily trace Gayatri. Only on landing in the city did he understand the enormity of the situation. The city was big and he had no leads or friends. All the money was spent in three days. As he wearily dragged himself along the road, he heard the familiar chant of the *mantras* from a wedding hall nearby. He was drawn towards it, feeling a strange kinship with the words.

***

Once the head *vadhyar* realized Hari knew all the *mantras* and rites, he took him in and assigned him small functions. He helped Hari find quarters in the *Veda patshala*[21]. Sometimes, as he lay in bed at night, Hari would think about his engineering college and his life in Palakkad.

He would smile sadly, thinking how his aunt tried to push him into becoming a *vadhyar* and how he had rebelled! Now he was exactly doing what she wanted. She had finally won. He had toyed with the idea of going back to Palakkad to finish his studies but pride stopped him. After settling in, Hari had tried to find Gayatri through her dad's bank. His visits to a few branches made him realize he had very little information about him.

❖❖❖

Hari soon became the most sought-after *vadhyar* in the city. The rest of the time he spent in dreaming about Gayatri. Unable to accept he had lost her, he assumed he had married her. He would talk to her throughout the day, telling her about his experiences and pretending she was always with him.

As he rose in his profession, people did try to suggest that he marry. The *vadhyars* spoke about various girls, cousins, friends' daughters, and neighbors. But Hari firmly refused.

❖❖❖

Today, as he performed her *shraddam* with a heavy heart, as he chanted the *mantras* for her journey to the other world, he carefully refrained from saying *muma*.

---

21 *Veda patshala* - A centre dedicated to teaching vedas.

HOTEL DILBAHAR

Rahul Bhattacharya opened the letter eagerly and reading it, let out a whoop of joy. It was from SMSG, giving details about his journey to Mumbai and his stay there.

Sur Milale, Sang Gaale or SMSG was a music reality show and the latest rage on television. He had been selected to represent the East zone and was sent tickets to go to the finale in Mumbai - the city of dreams.

"Maaaa[22].." he called out loudly.

He found her in Ridhima *maashi*[23]*'s* room. Subarna was sitting beside her sister's bed and doling out medicine. He waved the letter at them and yelled, "Yes yes yes! The finals of SMSG will be in Mumbai. Here is the letter with the tickets and all details". He went and sat beside Ridhima and taking her frail hands in his, said, "*Maashi*, this is all because of your encouragement. How I wish you were well enough to come to Mumbai with me!" Ridhima's hands suddenly slipped away from his and she averted her gaze from him. He thought he saw her eyes misting with tears. Subarna jumped up and hugged her son. "That is wonderful, Rahul! Let us call your father and give him the good news. We will have to decide which songs you need to brush up on."

---

22 *Maaaa* - Mother

23 *Maashi* - Mother's sister

Rahul knew that his mom was trying to keep him from seeing his aunt tear up. His parents and aunt always behaved this way whenever Mumbai was mentioned. He never knew why. He was born in Mumbai but his parents never referred to it. He came to know it only through his birth certificate. Hoping they wouldn't stop him from going to Mumbai, he thought of how SMSG had brought him into the limelight. Though his singing had fetched him prizes in school and college, he set his heart on the crowning glory at SMSG .

Being born into a family that lived by music had helped him grow as a singer. His father was a talented keyboard player who chose to train youngsters over performing. While his mother was a *Rabindra sangeet*[24] exponent, his sister Navya was a guitarist in a band. His aunt had even got a break to sing for Bollywood movies when she was younger. But she had left the industry suddenly and stopped singing except for humming a melody when she was in the mood - which was rare of late.

Now, he was the only one in the family who actually sang. Bollywood music, however, united all five and ruled conversations at the dinner table. The talk swayed between Asha Bhonsle versus Lata Mangeshkar and Mohammed Rafi and Kishore Kumar. It was never old songs against contemporary music because all of them stood by Hindi classics.

"Where is it going to be held? Will they be giving you accomodation? Does Navya know about this?" his mother's questions echoed her excitement.

---

24 *Rabindra Sangeet* - Songs written and composed by Rabindranath Tagore

As Rahul searched for his phone, Subarna lifted Ridhima and helped her sit straight and handed her a glass of water.

"Yes *pa*[25]. They have sent me tickets on the AC Duronto Express. *Haan*, hotel bookings too. Actually, this hotel is sponsoring all the singers. Yes...it is the Hotel Dilbahar near Marine Drive and…"

The conversation was broken by the sound of glass shattering, followed by a smothering silence.

Rahul looked up and noticed that both his mom's and aunt's faces had turned pale. When Subarna felt Rahul's stare, she bent down to pick up the glass shards. He went out to the terrace to finish his conversation. On hanging up, he climbed the ladder to the water tank and perched himself on it. Before long, he was trying to piece together all he knew about the family's and particularly his aunt's connection with Mumbai.

❄❄❄

Ridhima was his mother's sister. He always remembered her as a beautiful lady with sad eyes that lit up only when music was being discussed. He was close to her right from his childhood. His mother used to say that when he was a baby, he would stop crying as soon as his aunt picked him up. Her singing soothed him. She also was his first music guru.

He knew his Ridhima *maashi* had a dark secret buried in Mumbai. They had all left Mumbai because of it and she never spoke of her life in the city. One of few words,

---

25 *Pa* - Father

she went about her life quietly. The last one year saw her fall ill often and later, she was diagnosed with cancer. The doctors had given her only a few months to live.

He suddenly remembered a conversation he had overheard between his mother and *maashi* when he was just a small kid.

Subarna had been pestering Ridhima to agree to be 'seen' by a prospective groom.

"I think you should forget what happened in the past and get on with life," Subarna coaxed her sister.

"If it was just a past, I could have. But it is the guilt... the unrelenting guilt... I don't think I can get over that."

"What happened was only an accident."

"I wish I were so sure," Ridhima said with a finality.

By then, they had noticed him and continued to talk in whispers.

***

Navya was strumming the guitar lazily and humming to herself. Rahul sat next to her, lost in thoughts.

"Well Rahul, My advice to you is to fall in love."

"WHAAATTT!"

"You wanted ideas on how to bring a 'feel' to your singing, remember? The last time, all the judges unanimously agreed that while your singing was technically perfect, it lacked emotion. The songs you have chosen now are all about love. Fall in love and think about her to add the feel to your singing."

"Stop it, Navya! Be serious. I want to tell you what happened this afternoon." He described their mom's and aunt's reactions. "How much do you know about Ridhima *maashi*'s life in Mumbai?"

She stopped playing and told him what she knew, "Ridhima *maashi* had tried her hand at Bollywood and was poised to sing for a movie. But some tragedy struck and that shattered the charming vivacious girl she was. I couldn't find out what exactly happened but soon after that, everyone left for Kolkata and *maashi* has been living with us since then."

Rahul tried calculating his aunt's age and was surprised to realise that she must be only about 50 years old. Her serious outlook or the old-fashioned way of dressing, or maybe even the illness, made her look much older than 50, he surmised.

❖❖❖

Rahul got out of the train at CST Mumbai and looked around. The energy of the city took his breath away. While he was quite used to crowds, after all he was from Kolkata, this vibrancy was new to him. The crowd here was dynamic and constantly on the move. He let himself be guided by the crowd towards the exit. Putting the letter in his pocket for easy reference, he walked briskly and found his way to Hotel Dilbahar on Marine Drive.

As he waited in the lobby, he looked around in awe. A huge pillar at the centre of the ornate lobby held over a thousand photos of celebrity patrons. The 75-year-old hotel was Bollywood's favourite and pictures of actors from Prithviraj Kapoor to Aamir Khan and fearless Nadia to Priyanka Chopra adorned the pillar. Some smiled at the camera while others were in deep conversation. A few were caught unawares.

Starry-eyed, he went crazy identifying every actor. He looked around as if he expected Raj Kapoor or Waheeda Rehman to materialise out of thin air. He had to tear himself away from the photos when the receptionist called his name. As he got into the elevator, he wished his parents and Navya were with him to enjoy the experience.

❋❋❋

It was evening and Rahul lay on the bed, half asleep. A knock at the door heralded room service and the waiter came in rolling a trolley. He took out a brown colored bottle and some snacks and placed it on a side table with a couple of wine glasses.

"I didn't order anything, " Rahul objected.

Giving him a mysterious smile, the waiter said "Compliments from the hotel, sir," before closing the door behind him. Thirsty, Rahul checked the bottle. It was chilled but the label seemed old and the letters were smudged. "Vintage wine," he thought to himself and poured a generous measure from the bottle. The purplish-looking liquid gurgled and smelt a bit like cough syrup.

Sitting on the bed, he took a tentative sip. The liquid tasted good on his parched tongue and he gulped it all down. Suddenly, his head reeled, his throat burnt and he felt his whole body being squeezed. He fell back on the pillow and his last thought was "Will this spoil my throat and stop me from singing well for the finals?"

❋❋❋

Rahul woke up sweating and wondered what had happened to the AC. He looked around and realised he was not in the hotel room. On the verge of panic, he got up from the rickety old bed and tried the door. It opened and he walked out warily.

The place seemed to be some kind of a seedy hotel. There were a few people around, all dressed in clothes of yesteryears but no one noticed him. He walked down the staircase and reached the lobby and was shocked.

It was the same Hotel Dilbahar and the same lobby. There was the pillar in the centre but the surroundings belonged to a 60's film. He walked towards the pillar and saw that there were only 10-15 photos. He recognised V Shantharam, Nargis, Raj Kapoor and a few others.

He sat down in a chair and tried to make sense of what was happening to him. He had read about time travel in some books but dismissed it as imagination. It now dawned on him that the drink had transported him back in time, to the 50s or 60s going by the photos on the pillar. And the way people were bustling around and not taking any notice of him, he realised he was invisible.

Suddenly, there was a commotion and he saw someone enter the hotel. Oh My God! It was Dev Anand, looking very young and debonair. He was accompanied by some hangers-on. As they found seats, the waiters rushed to take their orders.

Dev Anand was narrating an incident. "... And I had a shooting in 10 minutes. So I tell the laundry guy that there is no other way... I'll wear this shirt and act. As I entered the location, I see the new choreographer, a young handsome guy called Guru Dutt, wearing my shirt! I go talk to him and realise that he had the same laundry guy." Laughter followed.

Rahul realised that Dev Anand was referring to how he first met Guru dutt, during the making *Hum Ek Hain* for Prabhat Film Company, in Pune. He recollected that they had become good friends later and Dutt went on to direct *Baazi*, a crime thriller starring and produced by Dev Anand. As per the actor's anecdote, Rahul pegged the year at 1945.

He looked around and saw that the room was filled with celebrities from the golden era of Bollywood. Euphoria marked his steps as he walked around identifying the celebrities, recalling gossip about them and committing to memory their attire and hairdos to tell his family. He wandered to the reception and saw a calendar there. 2-4-1945 it read.

All of a sudden, fatigue overcame him and he held the railings as he walked up to his room. Rahul fell on the bed and was soon lost to the world.

❖❖❖

Rahul woke up to find he was back in the 21st century. The hotel had arranged a tour of Mumbai for all the SMSG contestants. It was late when he returned from the sightseeing, full of the beauty of Marine Drive at night. He was about to turn in for the day when he remembered last night's adventure. He checked the small fridge in the room and sure enough, there was the bottle tempting him with its purplish liquid. He poured a little into a glass and took a hesitant sip. Nothing happened and he filled the glass halfway. Gulping it down, he felt the familiar burning sensation in his throat and crumpled onto the bed.

***

This time, he raced down the stairs to the lobby. First, he checked the date at the reception and saw that it was 4-11-1995. Next he checked the pillar and saw pictures of Shah Rukh Khan, Kajol, Madhuri Dikshit, Jackie Shroff and Juhi Chawla among the stalwarts.

He realised that the quantity of the liquid decided which era he landed in.

As he flitted around the tables and watched his favourite film people, he saw a group of young adults trooping in, laughing and talking. One of them, a pretty girl in a pink dress, looked familiar but he could not place her. He moved over to their table and listened in, knowing that they could not see him. The group ordered food and from the banter at the table, Rahul realised the pretty girl had a boyfriend who was to join them soon.

"My birthday and he is late. The men never realise how much a girl is hurt by this," she sulked.

A dark sombre-looking guy sitting next to her said..."So what? I am here with you. I will never disappoint you on your birthday. I will give you a special treat."

She turned towards him in irritation, "Pramod, you know how special Shivam is to me. No one can take his place. I have told you a hundred times. Go look for some other girl and stop pestering me."

It suddenly dawned on Rahul that the girl in the pink dress was none other than Ridhima *maashi,* much younger, prettier and more lively.

There was an embarrassed silence all around and another friend cajoled the girl, "Ridhima, give Shivam a break. He has gone to meet the great Dilip Mehta. Maybe your birthday is lucky for him and he will end up getting a role."

"Shivam is handsome and talented. He just needs the luck factor to land a role," she stood up for him before someone at the table yelled, "Hey there he is!"

Rahul turned around to see a dashing young man approaching them. There was something heartbreakingly familiar about his looks and expression. But for the life of him, Rahul could not place him. He went through the list of heroes of the period and still couldn't identify him.

Shivam announced that he had bagged the role and was immediately surrounded by the admiring friends and their numerous questions. He raised his hands dramatically and said, "Wait. First let me cool down my girl". He produced a bouquet of roses and bent to offer it, in filmy style, to Ridhima. Her pretense of anger soon gave way to a smile as she accepted the flowers.

As Rahul watched the scene unfold, a powerful emotion swept through him. He was able to get into Shivam's mind and feel and know what he was going through. He could feel everything - the great love Shivam had for the girl, the elation of having got his first break in Bollywood and his pleasure of being with his friends.

They congratulated him and there were some good-natured calls for a treat. Shivam ordered a round of drinks for everyone and after a while, all of them left except him and Ridhima. They held hands and walked up the five floors to the terrace. As Rahul hovered around them, he saw the beautiful view from atop the building. He could see the Marine Drive, a beautiful curve with lesser lights. There was a soft wind blowing from the Arabian Sea and a half-moon breathed magic into the setting.

Shivam had his arms around her and they were watching something down the road.

"Look", said Shivam, "Your sister and brother-in-law."

Ridhima peeked at them and took a step back. "Hope they didn't see me with you. This is the problem of meeting here. It is plumb in front of my house."

"So what?"

"First thing, they want me to sing for Bollywood films and make some money. My sister is going to have a baby soon and there is hardly any money at home. My brother-in-law has worked hard to get me contacts in the industry. So if they catch me romancing, they will be angry that I am distracted from my mission. Secondly, my sister is already in her last month of pregnancy and she gets tired fast. I have promised to be back home in time to cook dinner. I really need to go," Ridhima tried brushing his hands off.

"First, sing my favourite song for me. Then I'll let you go," Shivam pleaded.

She smiled softly at him and before long, the words found a melody on her lips.. *Tum mujhe yun bula na paoge...*

As her mellifluous voice sang the love song, Shivam was moved to tears. 'You will never be able to forget me so easily... Yes... you cannot forget me.... whenever you hear this song, you will always sing along...'

She finished the song and stood up to go. "You are going to meet the music director tomorrow ? What song are you singing," Shivam wanted to know.

"This same song of course. This is my masterpiece."

Jealousy choked Shivam. This was his song. She sang it so soulfully just for him. And tomorrow she would sing it in front of another man. Her eyes would shine with love and her voice sound magical but someone else would enjoy it.

"No way! I won't allow you to sing this song," he shouted.

"What do you mean? I have to impress him enough to give me a chance to sing. I have to sing my best and this is the song," Ridhima was firm.

"I have my friends in the industry. I will make sure you won't get a chance to sing for movies. I'll make sure you quit".

"I am not quitting. Do you have any idea how much I had to struggle to get this chance? You got the chance to act just today. If someone tells you to give it all up, would you be happy?"

"But I am not a beautiful girl and people cannot take advantage of me.. but you? So lovely that any man will be tempted by your beauty. I am not stopping you from singing. Just saying you should not sing for movies. Maybe you can give music lessons and do some stage shows."

"Music lessons? Earn some 30 rupees a month teaching uninterested kids pushed by keen parents? Don't you dare be condescending. Do you have any idea how much I will earn by singing playback? The money I am going to bring will help my family. You cannot stop me. I am going to the production house first thing tomorrow morning".

"Go by all means. I know for a fact that the production in-charge there is a womaniser. He is definitely not going to let go of a beautiful girl like you, especially if you go asking for a chance to sing".

"I have talent and my morals are good. You wait and see if I'll get the role on my own or not," Ridhima seethed.

Rahul began shivering all at once as the effect of the liquid wore off. He was reluctant to leave the place as he wanted to know what happened next. But he knew he had to leave. As he took the steps, he saw that someone had been watching Shivam and Ridhima all the while. He was sure that the guy was in the group of friends. Yes! His name was Pramod, he remembered. The man who was jealous of the bond between Shivam and Ridhima. But why was he watching them secretly? Rahul couldn't shake off the feeling that he had met this man recently, in Mumbai.

***

The next day was hectic with SMSG rehearsals. But how much ever he tried to put his heart into it, Rahul kept thinking of Shivam and Ridhima.

While he was trying to get the *raga* and the beats right, his mind compulsively wandered to the terrace; wondering if they made up or if they parted in anger. He felt the present was a dream. He felt more connected to the past.

He was exhausted by the evening. Once back in the room, Rahul did not hesitate before he drank the fiery liquid. To reach the same era, he had to pour the exact amount as the last time but that would be the last of the liquid. With a sigh, he poured it into a glass and drank it in a single gulp.

Rahul raced to the front desk and found the calendar. He had traveled to the very next day after the terrace episode. He was also slightly surprised and happy to note that that was the day he was born. He smiled to himself as he searched for Shivam and Ridhima in various rooms. But they were not to be found anywhere. Disappointed, he sat at a table.

He decided to check the terrace and saw that Shivam was alone, obviously waiting for Ridhima. There was a half smile on his lips and a jewel box in his hand. Reading his mind, Rahul realised Shivam was planning on proposing to her.

He felt that an important event was to unfold and he had a role to play when Ridhima entered.

As he heard her footsteps, Shivam hid the jewel box in a niche in the wall and pretended to be angry. Rahul admired his acting skills. Shivam had gone from excited to being angry in just a moment.

Ridhima walked up to him and asked angrily, "What? Pramod told me you wanted to talk to me. I am definitely going to meet the music director. I would have gone right in the morning, but there was a small family problem. As soon as it is sorted, I am leaving."

Shivam moved towards her slowly and deliberately, stood in front of her and said sternly, "No. You won't go. I am going to do something before you go. I have thought a lot about this. I know it is drastic and you may regret this. It may shock you into changing your mind. I have no other option. What I am about to do is going to change your life...maybe forever... so just think through before you…"

Ridhima glanced down from the terrace and let out a yell. "Oh! Shivam, I have to leave now. My sister is due today and looks like something is wrong. My neighbour is standing there with her and trying to cross over and reach the hospital. I have to go," she ran down.

Shivam's shoulders sagged in despair.

Rahul peeked from the terrace. He saw that Ridhima had reached down and was hugging her sister and consoling her. She held her sister's hand and helped her up the steps of the hospital. With a thrill, Rahul realised it was his mom down there and he was about to be 'born'.

He turned back to see that Shivam was broken. He had perched himself on the parapet wall. Pramod walked in and placed a hand on his shoulder. Shivam looked up at him and said, "Oh Pramod! I just wanted to scare her a little and then surprise her with the ring. I let her assume that I was talking seriously and hinted at suicide. I was planning to show her the ring when she rushed off to tend to her sister".

Pramod gave him a sympathetic pat on the shoulder.

"I wanted to surprise her and ask her to marry me. Not that I have a lot of money. But if she is married to me, then people will hesitate to take advantage of her. Also if my movie is a hit, then I'll have some say and I can get her more chances to sing. But she didn't even wait to hear. She must be thinking I was talking about suicide," Shivam lamented.

Pramod put his other hand across Shivam's shoulder in a consoling gesture but hatred burned in his eyes. He pushed Shivam and sent him flying over the wall.

Rahul rushed towards them but he was too late. As he watched, aghast, he felt Shivam's panic.

As Shivam fell, he was horrified that one of his own friends had done this to him. Then the terrible thought of Ridhima believing he had committed suicide. Guilt that he had put her in such a situation and hopelessness about being unable to assuage her guilt. Frustration about letting her in for a lifetime of contrition. A final inhuman panic about doing something to clear her self-reproach.

A shudder brought Rahul back to his senses and he saw that Pramod was not around. The coward.

With tears in his eyes, Rahul turned to leave the terrace when he was pulled towards the niche in the wall, where Shivam had hidden the jewel box. He did not know why but he was very sure that it was important that he take the box. He opened it to see a ring with the letters 'R' and 'S' entwined and set with small diamonds. As he put it into his pocket, his knees started wobbling and weakness defeated him.

Rahul was finally on his bed. The bottle lay on the table, empty. In his heart, he knew he would never be able to visit the past. He remembered how it started with a guy coming in with the bottle. As his eyelids drooped, he knew who Pramod was. He was the waiter who had brought him the liquid. In that moment before sleep took over, he understood Pramod wanted to be forgiven.

❖❖❖

The hall was filled to capacity. It was the finals of SMSG and Rahul was on stage singing *Haan tum mujhe yun bula na paaoge*. As the lyrics flew out of his mouth effortlessly, with practised ease, he put himself in Shivam's shoes and thought of his undying love towards Ridhima. The pathos of lost love and the sweet sadness of beautiful memories welled up in his voice. The melody wafted among the audience, overwhelming them.

❖❖❖

Navya picked up the phone on the first ring. "Heyyyyy Navyaaaaa! Oh My God! I have done it!I am on the top of the world! I am the SMSG superstar."

"I know Rahul, we were all watching. I am so happy for you. Hey how did you sing so soulfully? I felt you were singing about a girl. I have never heard you put so much depth into a song. It brought tears to even dad's eyes.. imagine…"

Navya had news for her brother. "Hey, yesterday *ma* finally broke down and was telling me about their life in Mumbai. When you were born, you showed no signs of life. Doctors couldn't get a heartbeat for almost a minute. Suddenly, there was a commotion outside the hospital and as if the loud noises disturbed you, you jerked all at once and started crying. But sadly, it also was the same day when *mashi's* boyfriend committed suicide and that created the commotion".

She continued to talk but Rahul had stopped listening. Finally, everything fell in place in his mind. He touched his pocket to feel the jewel box. He knew he had a mission to complete, entrusted to him by both Pramod and Shivam. He was to help Ridhima *mashi* know the truth and finally forgive herself.

WHY DIDN'T THE DOG BARK

Inspector Murugan came in with small styrofoam cups of hot ginger tea in both hands.

Detective Raj accepted a cup, sipped appreciatively and asked, "What did the station master say?"

"No hope. The derailment has stranded several trains. Our connecting train will hopefully come by tomorrow afternoon. Meanwhile there is nothing to eat in the canteen. So I just bought tea and some buns and two bananas. That's all for dinner".

Both of them were the only passengers resting in the 1st class waiting room of the sleepy little station. A man in a blue uniform walked past them and out through the gate, swinging green and red lanterns. The platform was deserted and appeared dismal, lit only with flickering 40 watt bulbs.

Swatting at the mosquitoes, Murugan said, "No chances of sleep. To while away the time, why don't you tell me about some cases you have solved?"

Raj thought for a while and suddenly clicked his fingers. "I know. I will tell you about this interesting Lonavala case and will give you all details, exactly as I had got them. Using them, you try and guess who the murderer is".

He put his feet up on the table and settled comfortably and Murugan pulled his chair closer and listened.

"First meet the characters."

❋❋❋

VISHAAL

I always knew I was different. Right from my childhood, I had realized, I had the flair for blackmailing. While still a kid, I could easily ferret out who hid their report cards from their parents and I learnt to pressure them into bringing me chocolates and gifts. I knew which kids stole from others' lunch boxes and made sure I got a share from them. I derived pleasure in pretending to tell on cheaters during exams. You see, I was not just a blackmailer; I was an artist. I enjoyed it when people were scared of me. The pleasure I felt when I saw sudden fear in people's eyes!

Did I grow out of it? Hell, no! If anything, I refined the art. I enjoyed torturing my blackmailees; yes I shall call them that. I love them. Hahaha… they are literally my life and blood as I live off the money they give me grudgingly. I lie on my bed remembering their fearful glances and feel happy.

Don't ask me how I could read secrets. It came to me as easily as bowling to boys and giggling to girls.

So now you see me... a young man about the town, well read and fed. Obviously a man of means but where do you think the money is coming from? From secrets. I have a long list of blackmailees. I can't be expected to do all the hard work. So, my four lieutenants do the dirty job of collecting the money. We meet once a month at one of their houses. I insist that the host provide dinner for all of us. I have good fun at these 'parties'.

It is no jolly party, trust me. I know they hate it. I also make sure they hate each other. I feed them lies about the others and watch them hate each other. Whenever we are all together, I love to see the fearful and hateful glances they give each other. They never want to linger. They come from different walks of society and hardly have anything common between them. So they stay only to give me the collection and want to get away, their hatred for each other showing on their faces. But I keep them around, taking pleasure in their discomfort, enjoying baiting them and feeding little lies to them...What? Did I hear the word sadistic? That I am and am proud of it... hahahahahaha...

❊❊❊

THERESA

I was born into a pious Catholic family. When I was 16, I fell in love with a classmate and even without realizing the significance, became pregnant. My parents, who lived like they were the pillars of the church, could not think of an abortion. You can only guess the struggle my parents went through. Even after 10 years, they haven't forgiven me. But they stood by me when I had the baby and deposited the bundle in an orphanage.

Later, I went to college and when I was 21, got married to the 'perfect' rich son-in-law my parents chose, Mr. Philips Varghese.

Of course we didn't tell Philips about the baby. He was a society man. Even a hint of a scandal and my life with him, in his spacious bungalow with indoor heated swimming pools, would be over. Anyways, I didn't want to hurt my parents any more. So I buried my secret deep in my mind and went on being the perfect Mrs. Varghese.

Life would have gone on but for the fact that I did not conceive even after four years of marriage. My maternal instincts went into overdrive and I began longing for a baby. One night, I had a dream. My baby, the little girl I had 10 years ago, was accusing me of abandoning her. Crying, she asked me how I could punish her for a crime I committed.

I approached the orphanage secretly, telling them I was planning to adopt. After some research, I found her. Then began my secret pleasure. I visited my 10-year-old girl, talked and laughed with her, helped her with her projects. But always as Theresa aunty. Not as her mother.

She was mine, biologically, but I had to meet her on the sly; all the while worried if Philips would find out.

Then, Vishaal entered my life.

The rascal! He somehow found out about my orphanage visits and my baby and started blackmailing me. Now I am in his clutches. I am paying him huge amounts periodically, unknown to my husband. Not only that, Vishaal has made me his assistant, which means I have to collect the money from his victims and hand it over to him once a month. There are three others besides me. All hateful losers! I don't know who I hate more, Vishaal or my colleagues.

I am always worried that Phillips may find out. How many excuses can I give for the huge withdrawals once a month? Add to it the monthly so-called 'meetings' with those wretched people.

I could put up with everything if only I could visit my baby once in a while. But this villain wants double the money if I go to the orphanage. Life is hell. Hope God will strike him down dead or someone will butcher him. I want the plague to get him. Oh Lord, have mercy on me... but I hate him with all my heart.

❊❊❊

NARESH AGARWAL

I am Naresh. Dr Naresh Agarwal. Successful neurosurgeon at Lohia Hospital and slated to be the Dean of the hospital. Haha. You guys think I am too young? Yes, I actually am. But I have an unblemished record and my very capable hands… these hands which can finely remove a tiny tumor without harming a single neuron. I am looking forward to being the youngest Dean of Lohia Hospital. Yes, there is competition from other senior doctors. After all, this is not only a privilege, but also there is a huge jump in the pay package.

Yes. It looks like I am slated for it except... except for Vishaal...that swine of a blackmailer!

Actually I was not born as Naresh Agarwal but I am Naresh Majetty. I see that some of you recognize the name and shudder. Yes, I am the son of Rajesh Majetty, the doctor who was a serial killer. The same scoundrel who killed his patients just because he enjoyed the feel and power of killing. The devil who killed up to 30 patients before the police found him. It was a sensational case for no one believed that a person of a noble profession could be a murderer.

Actually even though he is my father, we have hardly been under the same roof. He left my mother, his legally wedded wife, soon after I was born. So except for donating some genes, he has had nothing to do with my upbringing. But you know the reporters. My mom and I were hounded by the press to such an extent that when I was a kid, my mom got my name changed to Naresh Agarwal legally. Since then, no one associated me with serial killer Majetty.

That was until Vishaal came along.

I have been doling out huge amounts every month. A few months ago, he 'appointed' me as his lieutenant. Now like a bill collector, I have to collect all his dues. We all meet once a month at a very 'jolly' party. All the other three sorry faces also join. Even the meal is to be sponsored by one of us every month. Look at his villainy. I think he revels in our misery. Last week he asked for 10 crores. You heard it right. He threatened to make sure all the doctors on the panel got a copy of my original birth certificate with that hated person as my father. If that happens, the senior doctors will make sure I never ever work in Lohia Hospital, let alone become the dean.

I wish I could get at Vishaal with my scalpel. I would chop him up like a shredder and enjoy every chop. I hate him!

***

SAMIR HAZARIKA

Yes, I am the one and only gymnast from Assam to have represented India in the summer Olympics in London last year. Slated to represent the country in the next event in Rio, Brazil in 2016. Not just slated, but with luck, might even get a gold medal for India. You guys don't recognize me? Why am I not surprised? Sadly, such immediate recognition is reserved only for cricketers in India.

But the strange thing is, I was a cricketer to begin with, a promising opening batsman being considered for the Indian team.

It was the day I had to play in front of the selectors. You have to understand the pressure on a sportsman when he is under scrutiny and he knows it. So even though I had immense confidence in my skills, I took some performance enhancing drugs. But one of my own jealous teammates ratted on me and I was caught. Yes. It was a huge blow not only to my family and me, but to the whole Assam cricketing community.

Luckily, they helped me keep this news away from the media after I vowed to never play cricket. I guess they also wanted it that way so that the state was not shamed. Anyway I spent the next few years training to be an athlete; once a sportsman, always one. So I excelled in my second choice and have risen up to this level. I have strictly and sincerely kept clear of drugs and my life could have become another success story but for Vishaal.

He somehow uncovered the secret and has been threatening me ever since. I know that it was my only mistake and am confident about my talent. But the story would rob me of all credibility in India where heroes are made and broken by the press; I will become a pariah and be termed a 'has been'. Let alone going to Brazil, I will be happy if I could get to give away prizes in high schools.

What else to do? I have been paying and to torture me further he has made me his lieutenant. More than collecting money from small-time criminals, it pains me to be associated with the other lieutenants. I hate the whole lot of them. I know they call me the druggie.

One of these days I would love to kill Vishaal with my bare hands.

SHANTHA DURGA PANNADI

I am Shanta, a junior secretary in the ministry of social justice. Having been born in a *dalit*[26] family, I can say with pride that I did well in school and college and rose to this level in the ministry through sheer hard work and luck. Life was easy because of the reservations.

I am reserved by nature and I don't mix with people easily. My parents passed away and I live a quiet life by myself in my government quarters in Mumbai. My plans for the future were simple. I was thinking of finding a suitable dalit boy and marrying him.

Suddenly, my life turned topsy turvy when I met this hated person, this villain, called Vishaal. I don't how he found out, but he did.

---

26 *Dalit* - A member of the lowest caste as per the traditional Indian caste system

I was actually born as a *Brahmin*[27] girl and named Shantha Lakshmi Iyer.

I was mediocre in studies and also my family was poor. *Appa*[28] had a friend who worked for the local municipality office and he offered to get me a certificate stating I was born a dalit. *Appa* only wanted me to do better and go to good schools and colleges. So he paid his friend some money after selling our small hut. With the caste certificate, we moved to a new city and started the life of a dalit family.

I had even forgotten that I was born a Brahmin. Except for fabricating my caste, I have a clear conscience. If Vishaal had not found out, I would have settled down to domestic bliss with a suitable boy. All my dreams shattered because of him.

As long as I gave him some money every month, it was not so bad. But he made me something called lootin... Leutin... Something like that. Then I had to collect money from other people he blackmailed and give it to him every month and I simply hated it.

But he made me do it saying that if I didn't, he would expose me and I would lose my job and social standing. Also no good boy would ever marry me.

I hate the other lootinous even more than I hate Vishaal. They all are nice rich people and they make me feel small and poor. I don't have parents, relatives or friends who can talk to this bad man and release me. I am

27 *Brahmin* - A socially and culturally superior person as per the caste system

28 *Appa* - Indian variant for father

all alone in the world and very sad. I light the lamp daily and ask God for Vishaal to be killed somehow. That's all I can do.

❖❖❖

Murugan didn't even swat the mosquito on his wrist. He was completely engrossed in Raj's tale.

"Continue", he said.

"Now that you know the characters, let me tell you what happened on that day".

He took a sip of the bottled water and continued.

"That day, it was Hazarika's turn to host the meeting. He had a huge bungalow in Lonavala. So he decided to have the so-called party there. Normally, they all met to just give Vishaal the money and hung around uncomfortably till they had the food and left as soon as they could.

But this time, as the venue was in Lonavala, some two hours from Mumbai, the party was supposed to be at night and everyone had to spend the night in the bungalow.

Hazarika had a cook, Menon. He had made some *biriyani* [29]and *raitha*[30] for the dinner. Everyone got a glass of lime juice as a 'welcome' drink. As they arrived one by one and took their seats, Menon offered them the drink.

---

29 *Biryani* - A blend of rice and meat or vegetables, seasoned with spices

30 *Raitha* - A yoghurt-based dish with cucumber and other chopped vegetables, usually an accompaniment with biryani

So, let us see how they all arrived. Prompt and punctual as always, Durga reached first. She held the glass of juice and sat uncomfortably for a while, trying to make conversation with a bored and irritated Hazarika. Then Vishaal arrived, followed by Theresa and both took their seats. Vishaal kept the conversation going and pitted both of them against each other. It was getting quite late and Dr Agarwal had not yet arrived.

By then, Vishaal became unusually sleepy. So he collected the money brought by the three of them and put it into a bag. He told Hazarika he did not want dinner and went to sleep in the bedroom downstairs. He gave orders that when the doctor arrived, he was to leave his collection in the same bag, which he had placed on a table next to his bed.

The cheerless party went on. Realizing his duty as a host, Hazarika tried to get them interested in his Assamese sword collection displayed in the drawing room. But they were all restless and one by one, all of them drifted to their allocated bedrooms on the first floor.

In the morning Durga had to leave early. So she came down and happened to glance towards the bedroom.

She let out a piercing scream and the other three rushed in and saw that Vishaal lay on the bed with an Assamese knife sticking out of his chest and congealed blood all over his shirt and body".

❋❋❋

Murugan got up, stretched himself and drank some water. A bell tolled somewhere. A cool breeze blew into the room. The bananas lay there uneaten. He returned to his chair.

Raj continued, "Next, let us look at the doctor's report on Vishaal's death".

DR SHRAVANTHI

I was called to confirm Mr.Vishaal's death in the early hours of January 13, 2013. I examined him physically. He had essentially died of multiple stab wounds. After I received the forensic reports, I could form a proper idea of what must have happened:

Mr. Vishaal had been administered a sleeping pill by about 8 pm on January 12. The slow acting drug made him uncontrollably sleepy by 10.30. PM. So he must have been in deep sleep by 10.45 pm. So when he was stabbed by about midnight, he could not have even uttered a cry. That is only the way, a strong man like him, could have been killed by someone of a smaller stature. He had been killed by a strong right-handed person.

My first impression was that whoever killed him had a lot of hatred and anger against him. The killer had driven the knife into Vishaal's body with so much force that it had ripped open the mattress below. There was no resistance from the victim but despite that, it is not very easy.

I would guess it was done by a physically strong person. On the other hand, a person of smaller stature, but highly motivated by hatred, could also have done it.

NAIR

I was cutting vegetables for *biriyani*, when Durga madam arrived. So I took the lime juice, which I had already made and left in the fridge, poured a glass and gave it to her on a tray. She took it and went and sat in the hall with my boss on the sofa and was talking to him. I started cutting the onions for the *raitha*, when Vishaal sir and Theresa madam came one after the other. When I was about to pour the lime juice, Durga madam said the onion smell would get into the juice and she poured the drink for both of them. I went back to the cutting board on the other side of the kitchen. I did not see what she did after that.

They all finished their dinner at about 10pm and were watching some movie. I finished clearing up and cleaning the kitchen by 11 pm and went to sleep in my room, which is at the back of the house. I woke up in the morning and was drinking tea when I heard the commotion and came running to the house.

❋❋❋

Raj lowered his legs from the table slowly, stretched his body to relieve the tension. Murugan offered him a banana but Raj refused. Murugan ate both and tried to find a garbage can. Raj joined him and they took a small walk on the platform and finally found one near the canteen. Then they settled down on a bench on the platform.

"Did you ask each of the four, if they did it?"Murugan asked.

"Yes, of course".

THERESA

Me kill Vishaal? Are you kidding! Have you seen his size and mine?

Inspector, do you seriously think this 'small' me could murder him? Did you hear what the doctors said? A few of the blows were so forceful that the bed below him had been ripped open.

Yes, no doubt I am happy and relieved. Now I can keep my secret trysts with my baby and still live the comfortable and rich life of Mrs. Theresa Phillips. But I did not commit the murder. Maybe you are barking up the wrong tree. What about that smug and conceited doctor guy? See how strong he is. I think he is capable of doing it. In fact, the more I think, the more I am convinced it is him.

NARESH AGARWAL

No way! God knows I had justified anger and reason to kill him. Actually, a part of me wishes it was true that I had killed him with my bare hands. I would definitely have derived immense pleasure.

Ohhh. I know you will not believe it without evidence. But look at the doctor's report. An unbiased doctor's report that is... Vishaal was given a sedative that would take at least one hour to act. And by some sheer luck, I got held by traffic and I came in after he went to the bedroom. That means whoever premeditated his murder had already given him the sleeping pills mixed with his drink much before I arrived on the scene. So that lets me out sir. He was sleeping in the bedroom when I came. So I placed my collection in a bundle on his bedside table. I would have loved to have gone back home but I had to spend the night there.

I think you guys should check the credentials of that sports guy. Did you all know he was a junkie? These junkies always have tremendous physical power when they are under drugs. Who knows! Maybe he filled himself with some "killing performance enhancing drugs" and committed the murder?

SAMIR HAZARIKA

You must be joking! Though the bugger was just asking for it, believe me. How he would goad all of us! Whoever did it, they have my good wishes. They have wiped out the plague. But I am not the murderer. Check with everyone who knows me. I am definitely left-handed. You can see videos of my cricketing days.

But did you ask that hillbilly if she did it. She is a devious one, believe me. She sits silently with that smug look on her face. These *paharis* have a lot of strength. Maybe she put the knife into him and is pretending she doesn't understand what you are asking her. She does that often. If the question does not please her, she says, "Please, I no understand. Can you ask two times?" Seriously, you must counter check her statements.

SHANTHA DURGA PANNADI

No...No...No... I did not kill him. It is the truth that I wanted to. Maybe because daily I pray to God, He killed him?

Do you think police also will think that I killed him? Ohhhh...But wait... wait for a minute. I found the dead body no? If I killed, I would not have found it...Correct no? I would be quiet and left for Mumbai and someone else would have found it...Correct no? I did not kill him though I am very happy that I don't have to give him money every month.

Maybe that Christian girl did it. She looks very weak, I know. She is very worried her stupid husband will come to know and when people are worried, they get a lot of strength. Or maybe she paid rent to one man and made him kill Vishaal? After all, she and her husband have much money... Big car... Yes. I think that is what happened. She give money to man in mask. He come in night and kill and run away. And you asking poor *pahadi*[31] girl if she killed.

NAIR

Nyaano[32]*?* Why should I kill him? I had not even met him. Hmmm...Yes...No... I mean I had gone with Hazarika sir once to one party and saw him there. Then I saw him next the night he was murdered but I did not kill him.

❖❖❖

Raj looked at Murugan, "Do you have any idea who did the killing?"

"I have some more questions".

"Where did the knife used for the crime come from?"

"Mr. Hazarika was from Assam and he had some ceremonial knives decorating the wall of his hall. The knife used to kill Vishaal came from that set. Theresa had asked about them during the dinner and Hazarika had taken just one from the set and showed it to the guests.

---

31 *Pahadi* - An ethnic group of the Himalayas

32 *Nyaano* - "Me?" in Malayalam

He then left it on the table. He did not remember putting it back. Neither did he notice any one of them show particular interest in the knife, nor did he see them taking it".

"What about the fingerprints on the knife?"

"It had fingerprints of all the four suspects and also Menon's. But then they all handled it when Hazarika showed it to them and Menon insisted he cleaned them regularly".

"Could anyone from outside the bungalow have done the murder?"

"Hmm... Hazarika has a dog and all the four suspects were sure they heard it bark. None of them were very sure of the time. They all agreed that it was after they went to bed, which was at about 12. However, Menon steadfastly said the dog did not make any unusual sounds the whole night. But Hazarika said Menon, a sound sleeper, may not have heard even a bomb explosion. However Menon is adamant that the dog did not bark".

"Did the police try to trace the sleeping pills?"

"Yes. They did. Nowadays it is difficult to buy sleeping drugs off the counter. So on checking around, they found only one relevant purchase. There is a medical shop near Theresa's house and the chemist there confirmed that she had bought 2-3 strips. But Theresa did not even deny it. It seemed she was having some insomnia problems from some time and she had the prescriptions too".

"Did Menon have any reasons to hate Hazarika or Vishaal?"

"Menon had been asking for a raise and Hazarika had not given it. But that was not enough for him to hate his boss. Anyway it was not Hazarika who got killed".

"Maybe Hazarika offered money to Menon and asked him to kill Vishaal."

"On checking through Menon's bank accounts for any unusual activities, we found no deposits but huge regular withdrawals. The withdrawals were dated before the murder. No unusual deposits or withdrawals after the murder date".

"What happened to the money all the suspects had handed over to Vishaal?"

"The money was placed in a suitcase and left at Vishaal's bedside. But after the murder was discovered and the police were called in, the suitcase was found empty. The four suspects said they had no idea who took it or where it went. Menon also said he did not know anything about it".

Murugan got up from the bench and began pacing about. Still frowning, he stopped and asked Raj, "May be an outsider entered the bungalow… the dog barked ... he saw the money lying next to the sleeping Vishaal, took the knife from the hall, went into the room, killed him and took the money."

"Then why did the dog stop barking?"

Murugan continued to walk. Suddenly, he stopped, clicked his fingers and said, "Maybe Menon was the guy with whom Theresa had a kid. Maybe he killed Vishaal so his ex-girlfriend could be freed from his clutches".

Raj calmly smiled and said, "Menon is 50 and Theresa is 26 years old".

A clock somewhere struck 4.

Murugan came and sat next to Raj, "I can't think how any one of them could have done it unless…" his voice rose with excitement, "unless all of them did it together."

"There. You got it. The murder was not done on the spur of the moment, in sudden anger, but it was well planned and neatly executed. It was done by all four suspects together".

"How exactly was it done?"

"Yes they formed an unholy-unlikely-alliance to get rid of their tormentor. I won't say they were not justified. Vishaal had been making their lives miserable and none of them were hardened criminals. Dr Agarwal planted the idea. He had seen through Vishaal's plan of making them hate each other. There is poetic irony in the fact that they used this very point to kill him at the monthly meeting he had formed to torture them.

Dr Agarwal explained to everyone that by joining hands, they could get away with the perfect murder, where each of them had an alibi.

So Theresa provided the sleeping pills and Durga mixed it with Vishaal's drink. Dr Agarwal was careful to come to the party only after Vishaal would have slept, thereby giving himself an alibi. Menon went to bed at 11 pm, after cleaning up. Then at about 12, Hazarika took the knife from the table and they all walked to the bedroom downstairs. Each of them struck two blows each so they wouldn't know whose thrust actually killed Vishaal.

This way they all stayed united in their crime and could not tell on each other. The case against Hazarika was loaded. After all, the murder took place in his bungalow, the knife used was his and also, he was physically capable. So to counter that, Dr Agarwal made a right-handed deep thrust so that Sameer, who was left-handed, could have an alibi. Also, Theresa's small stature cleared her.

On the day of the murder, by a strange coincidence, they came to know that Menon was also being blackmailed by Vishaal. In fact, Menon had been pestering Hazarika for a raise exactly for that. So the four of them were worried that he had a motive and would get caught for a crime he had not done. They had to do something immediately and Dr Agarwal came up with the dog barking idea. That opened doors for an outsider to have committed the crime and then removed the money from the suitcase. All of them took what was theirs so that the outsider theory would be strengthened".

❖❖❖

A rooster crowed somewhere, announcing the sun's ascent in the east.

HOUSE ON TIGER HILL

Geetha happily skipped down the last few steps. The small but cosy cottage was on Tiger Hill Road in Coonoor, a sleepy little town near Ooty.

She made up her mind about taking the house. She was in love with it! There was a small living room with a piano (yes!) just near the staircase. The dining room with chandeliers, a kitchen with lots of storage, a door leading into a garden - all made for a nice place to live in.

True that the garden was all dry and neglected but once she moved in, she would nurture it back to life, after all she had all the time in the world.

She had lost her husband two years ago.With a loving husband by her side, Geetha was planning on having a child. She had always loved kids.

But fate was cruel and her husband's demise shifted the focus from family to livelihood. Beyond a few thousands in her savings account, she did not have much money. With great difficulty, Geetha got his job on compassionate grounds. But the only vacancy was in Coonoor. So she had to find a place to stay in the new town till she was given a transfer back to Chennai. "And live here all alone," she thought, but pushed away her sad thoughts determinedly.

She peered into the house once again before the agent locked it up. As they both walked up the road, she asked him about the owners and how soon she could move in.

Baskaran Menon, the agent, did not reply immediately. She sensed a problem. She had to hurry to keep up with him and the steep roads of Coonoor made her breathless. They got into the jeep and once she caught her breath, she told him frankly, "I love the house and am keen on taking it. In fact, among all the houses you showed, I like this the best."

Menon concentrated on driving. She asked him once again, a little firmly, "What is the problem? Are they asking for a very high rent?"

"4,000 rupees".

"What! I can't believe it! All the other ones we saw today, though much smaller, cost twice. Why is the rent so low?" Menon smiled and continued to drive.

❋❋❋

A week passed and Geetha was still looking for a house.

"Thanks a lot for showing me so many houses. But I cannot forget that house on Tiger Hill Road. I know there is a problem. But please tell me about it and let me decide if I can take it."

Menon looked at her with sharp eyes. He liked what he saw. She must be around 30 but could pass off for a 25-year-old. She had wise grey eyes that had known sadness but were smiling at the world now.

He closed the pen and leaned back in his chair. "The house is supposed to be haunted. I don't know whether you remember the Anjana kidnap case of Coimbatore. A four-year-old was kidnapped by the maid and hidden away."

Geetha remembered the incident. It occurred three years ago. The photos of the child were in every newspaper; a pretty and vivacious child, Geetha recollected. The maid needed money urgently and had hidden the child somewhere and asked for 20 lakhs in ransom. The parents were more than willing to part with the money but the police became involved. When the maid came to collect the money, there was some firing and she was killed on the spot, before she could tell them where she had hidden the kid.

Then there were frantic searches all around Coimbatore but the child was never found. After some time, the public lost interest in the case.

Menon continued, "The maid knew someone in Coonoor. She had come to know that this house was vacant and the owners lived in the USA. So she hid the kid here.The maid had looked after Anjana ever since she was a baby. She was attached to the kid and had taken good care of her. When she went to collect the money, she had impressed on the kid that she must not step out of the house or cry loudly. The maid thought that as soon as the money was in her hands, she would let people know where she had hidden Anjana and then disappear. But fate had other plans."

After pausing for a minute, Menon continued, "Meanwhile, the child waited for her *nani*[33] to return.. She didn't dare cry or step out of the house. She must have eaten what was left and survived for a few more days."

"I came in bringing a prospective tenant and found her frail little body on the steps inside the house. She must have lain there, sobbing her little heart out; not knowing why her parents or her *nani* did not come for her, laid there till the last breath left her young body."

Menon's voice became hoarse and he pretended to cough to hide it. "Three months after that, a family came to stay but left in 10 days after they kept hearing a small kid cry."

"What does the ghost do?" Geetha was curious.

"Nothing. It just keeps crying. But you know how people are superstitious. So no one has been living in the house for one year. There is a caretaker who cleans the place once a week. That is all. I have told you everything, you can decide if you still want the house".

"Let me think about it. I'll let you know tomorrow".

❖❖❖

Geetha sat on her bed, pondering. Only 4,000 rupees rent meant that she could double her savings. Once back in Chennai, it would be difficult to save much because of the high cost of living. But what about the ghost?

There was no history of ghosts harming innocent people, she thought. Even movies showed them taking

33 *Nani* - Generally means grandmother but also used to refer to someone elderly

revenge only on those who had harmed them. She remembered reading that gods and ghosts were almost the same. No one has ever seen them. Only their effects had been felt by people - benevolent in God's case and malevolent in ghosts' case. Like Casper the friendly ghost, this one may be good, she smiled to herself.

❖❖❖

All the shifting and moving in exhausted Geetha. Menon was a big help. While leaving, he offered his wife's company for the night but she smiled and refused. As soon as her head hit the pillow, she drifted off to sleep.

Soon, her eyes opened. She was sure something had disturbed her. She checked the time and noted it was around 1 am. She sipped from a bottle of water on the side table and lay back. Then she heard it.

It was eerie. A small child crying her heart out. The grief affected her greatly. Her own tragedy of her husband's death had suddenly made her lonely and vulnerable. The kid's sobs brought her own sorrow to the front. She buried her head into the pillow and wept inconsolably.

❖❖❖

A week had passed after she moved into the house and she had heard the sobs daily around midnight. The first few days, she was frightened and covered her head with the bedsheet. She lay silently but tears tinged with a little fear rolled down her cheeks.

The last two days, she had sat on the bed and listened to the sobs, thinking about how scared the kid must have been; the loneliness and hunger she must have felt. Slowly, a deep pity towards the kid welled up in her and fear was replaced with sympathy.

Geetha was determined to get out of her bed the next time the crying began.

She lay in bed, tossing and turning.How will the so-called ghost react to her? Will it ignore her or harm her? A slight shiver went down her spine.

She first heard the cries around 12.30. Standing on unsteady legs, she opened her bedroom door without making a sound. Tiptoeing, she made her way towards the hall. She felt that the sobs were coming from the last of the steps which led to the bedroom upstairs. When she walked towards it, the crying stopped. There were small hurried sounds as if a kid caught being naughty was scampering away. She waited for a long time but didn't hear anything.

For a week, Geetha heard the same scurrying sounds as soon as she entered the hall.

❖❖❖

Today, all was silent. As soon as she neared the staircase, the crying stopped. She felt Anjana watching her, to see what she would do. Geetha sat down on the rocking chair near the steps and rocked back and forth, humming some tunes.

She woke up in the morning, on the rocking chair, with a sore neck. Her body was aching but her heart was on a song; happy that the 'ghost' had not harmed her, happy that it did not run away from her.

❖❖❖

A new routine had been set now. She would not sleep in the bedroom, she would sit on the rocking chair, reading or going through office files. Around midnight, she heard footsteps on the steps and knew it was Anjana. Geetha would keep the books aside and talk to Anjana as if she were a real four-year-old.

She could feel Anjana moving around her; sometimes she could sense her sitting on the last step. Once, she sang a song for her and felt Anjana very near her, almost touching her feet.

❖❖❖

As she got up from her office cubicle, Geetha realised that she was actually looking forward to the night. Five months had passed since she moved to the house. She enjoyed a deep sense of peace and happiness which she hadn't felt in a long time. Maybe Anjana had brought her maternal instincts alive or... maybe ghosts could sense love.

"Why not?" Geetha thought. "According to movies, if revenge and hatred can be felt by ghosts, why not love?"

On a whim, she went to a toy shop and bought a yellow, red and blue ball the size of a melon.

That night, as she sat on the rocking chair waiting for Anjana, she had the ball in her lap. As soon Geetha felt her near, she dropped it at her feet. Nothing happened for a while.

Then there was a joyous whoop and the ball kept moving around, as if it was being repeatedly kicked. Geetha was thrilled. All these days, she doubted if she was imagining the footsteps and the cries.

As the ball kept rolling madly, Geetha heard a chuckle, a happy one. That she could change the heartrending sobs to delightful laughter - Geetha was thrilled. That she could also forget her own tragedy and loneliness and learn to be content with the company of a kid,"even if it is a ghost kid" she thought to herself.

❖❖❖

Anjana had a naughty side too.

Once Geetha had fallen asleep on the chair and didn't wake up when Anjana entered. The ball was thrown at her face with full force and she woke up with a start, to howls of laughter. Geetha pretended to be angry and kept the ball on her lap. The footsteps went all around her but she didn't budge.

Suddenly, everything went quiet. Geetha looked all around her, trying to sense what was happening when the ball was pulled out of her lap, accompanied by a giggle.

❖❖❖

The idyllic life was hers for a year and then came the blow. Geetha was transferred back to Chennai.

She was heartbroken. She had put away all her unhappiness and made a good life for herself. Now, she had to give it all up. More than herself, she was worried for the kid - Anjana had learnt to love her and played with her. She too was dependent on her.

What would happen when she leaves? The sobs would be be heard again. Would SHE be the cause now? Will Anjana feel forsaken? Geetha did not want to think about it.

She tried to explain to Anjana one night that she had to go away. The ball suddenly stopped moving. Except that, there was no other indication if Anjana had understood.

Appetite and sleep eluded her. How could she explain her predicament to someone? The head office thought she was happy with the transfer. After all, she had initially been after them for posting in Chennai. She did not know how to explain that she did not want to go back.

❋❋❋

The day finally arrived. The office peon had helped her load all her things into the car.

She stood near the rocking chair and waited for Anjana but could not feel her at all. She walked on the stairs but the small feet did not join her there. She lingered for a while and finally with a long sigh, went out of the house.

The driver was waiting for her in the car and she opened the trunk to check if all her things were there.

Suddenly, the yellow-blue-red ball bounced up and caressed her cheeks. Then she heard a small excited giggle.

THE TANZANITE

Radha Sundaram kept her novel down and picked up the phone at the first ring, after noting that it was her friend Vimala calling. She was a reporter for a popular Mumbai-based film magazine.

Even before Radha said hello, the caller said "Radha, listen. You remember Minal Mulchandani? That theatre owner Hari*bhai*[34]'s wife whom we met at the *holi*[35] bash?"

"Hmmm... can't remember exactly, but tell me more".

"Remember, she once asked if your husband could take a packet of goodies to her sister Sheetal who studies in Delhi? Your husband delivered the package. I also remember you telling me that Sheetal showed a lot of attitude".

"Now I remember. My poor husband was scandalized that Sheetal met him in shorts and a skimpy top. So Minal wants another packet delivered?"

"No. No deliveries for Sheetal as she is here in Mumbai, at her sister's house, happily chewing up packets and packets of gum. I wonder if she is trying to give up smoking".

---

34 *Bhai* - Brother in Hindi

35 *Holi* - Celebrated as the festival of colours in India

"Ohhh…did she finish her fashion designing course then?"

"No. I heard gossip that she had some boyfriend trouble and that's why she gave up Delhi and is living with her sister here. Anyway, that's not my concern. But yes, someone else needs your help".

"Okay. If the famous Vimala is asking for my help, it must be interesting. Tell me".

"Yesterday, Minal threw a kitty party at their swanky new apartment in a suburban high-rise. She had invited a few close friends. One of the guests, Tara Mulchandani, came to the party wearing a brand new ring with a rare stone from Africa".

"Yes I know Tara. She is that jewellery shop owner's wife, isn't she? What did she do with her African ring?"

"She lost it Radha. I was there the whole time. I just can't understand how it simply vanished".

"Vanished? Not stolen? So how can I help? I thought the police would have been called in!"

"No one wants the police as everyone is worried about newspapers and scandal. That's when I thought of you. You are a logical person with sound common sense. If anyone can find out how it was lost, it is you. Remember how you helped me when my maid went missing. So, I am sending Tara to you".

***

Radha opened the door. Tara Mulchandani stood there, fidgeting with her bangles. She wafted off an expensive perfume. She was wearing a rich embroidered brocade *anarkali*[36], quite unsuitable for Mumbai weather. She carried a tiny purse embellished with golden threads and bells.

"Come in. Vimala just told me about your problem".

Tara sat on the sofa, unsmiling and not answering her.

"Can I get you some hot filter coffee? Or maybe some *masala chai*[37] and Kerala chips?"

Tara still did not answer.

So Radha just waited patiently.

Tara cleared her throat finally and said "You know Radha, I have always admired your smartness. I know you are a little different from all of us with your intellect. I have noticed that you easily win all the games we play. Plus all those books you read all the time".

Radha waited knowing fully well that Tara will come to the point soon.

"You know that film-theatre owner, Hari*bhai*? Minal is his wife and they moved into our apartment complex recently. We have formed a circle and it is full of her friends from the movie industry. All ultra-rich and famous socialites. So, yesterday we had a kitty party at their place".

---

36 *Anarkali* - A long dress of sorts with a well-defined bust and waistline and gathers flowing down in the shape of an umbrella
37 *Masala chai* - A variant of tea blended with spices

Tara seemed to hesitate for a while and lowered her voice, "What I am going to tell you now must remain a secret. You can't even tell it to Mr. Sundaram. I know you are good at keeping secrets. That is one of the reasons I have come to you".

After being duly assured that she has done the right thing and Mr. Sundaram was definitely not going to learn of it through her, Tara continued, "You know my husband Vivek has a diamonds and gold shop in Zaveri Bazaar. Recently, Mehul, a friend of his who had come from Tanzania, brought a rare and precious Tanzanite ring, set in platinum, to be given to his fiancée during their engagement. Mehul brought it home when he came for dinner and I absolutely fell in love with the dark violet stone set in the middle of tiny sparkling diamonds. It is supposed to be worth a crore. I secretly put it on my finger, took a photo on my mobile and sent it on Whatsapp to all my friends saying it was a gift from Vivek.

Mehul left it in Vivek's safe at the shop, so he could take it on the day of his engagement. I had meant to tell everyone it was a joke the next day. But all of my friends were so impressed by the ring and so envious that I let them think it was mine".

Tara waited and collected her thoughts. "But the next day, Minal called to inform me of the kitty party at her place next weekend and insisted that I wear the ring. I was afraid they would ridicule me if I didn't, and it had gone too far for me to admit it was not mine.

I went to our shop when I was sure Vivek would not be around and told the manager I wanted to see some of the latest designs in the safe. He opened it for me and I took out the Tanzanite ring and hid it in my purse and walked out after thanking him, very sweetly".

Tara could not meet Radha's gaze and lowered her eyes. After a while, she seemed to gather herself, "I had the desired effect. When I entered wearing it, almost everyone crowded around me to admire my ring…but...but... I lost it. And right this morning, Mehul called my husband and said he wanted the ring tomorrow. I know if my husband finds it gone, he will easily find out it was me. I just can't bear for him to know that I stole it and now lost it. Also it will be a big blow for him to admit to Mehul that it is missing. And he will have to shell out one crore! I know I have made a total mess of this".

"But why come to me? I am sure the police will be able to do a better job and find it for you".

"Oh no! Not the police. Firstly there will be a big scandal as the room was full of socialites. It is sure to get into the newspapers. Vivek is very reserved and he will hate to be in the middle of all the attention. Also, how will he face Mehul? That's when Vimala told me you helped her find her maid, who went missing. So please please help me?"

"Hmm…okay. I will surely try. But you will have to truthfully tell me everything I want to know".

Tara nodded." Firstly, describe everyone who attended the party".

"There was Minal, who was the host. She is in her late 20s and just had a baby. She looks good and dresses well. Her younger sister, Sheetal, has come down from Delhi.

She is doing a course in fashion designing. She is forever chewing gum and looking down on people".

"Who else?"

"Then there was Zara!"

Tara waited for Radha's response.

"Ohhhh. Zara? That aspiring starlet who was in the news recently for offering to strip if the Indian cricket team won?"

"Yes. The very same. She claims she did it to get noticed by the directors. She wanted a role or at least an item number".

"Okay. Next?"

"Then there was Vimala. You know her. She attends all important parties so that she can write the gossip for page 3. She always is a little aloof, to show that she is not one of us. But she enjoys the gossiping sessions and the food just like us".

Radha smiled. She knew that Vimala loathed the party ladies. She listened to gossip so she could do her job as the page 3 reporter. But yes, food was a weakness. And it showed in her ample frame.

"Did Nancy also attend? That cricketer's wife? I know she is on Minal's friend circuit?" Radha wanted to take the discussion forward.

"Oh, you know her?"

"Yes. Her husband Marshal was in the news recently for his involvement in the match fixing scam," Radha said.

"She is a regular in the circle. I don't know if this will help, but she is in need of money. She has not been contributing to the parties since 3-4 months".

"Oh. I will note that."

"Then there was Hema, my most trusted friend. She is very quiet and always smiling. She never has any opinions of her own. She agrees with everything everybody says. She has never had a fight," finished Tara.

"So there were seven people in all. Yourself, Minal, her sister Sheetal, Zara the starlet, Vimala the reporter, Nancy the cricketer's wife and the quiet Hema, your trusted friend.

Now describe in detail everything that happened from when you entered to till when you lost the ring".

"As I entered, everyone surrounded me, taking a look at my ring and exclaiming over it, complimenting me and telling me how lucky I was.

Nancy asked me to take it out, so she could see it better. So reluctantly, I took it off and handed it to her. She looked closely at the piece, remarking about its beauty. By then Minal came in from the kitchen, wiping her hands on a towel, and took it to admire. Then the maid called her for something and she gave it to Zara and left. Zara tried to put it on her finger but as she is small in stature, it was too loose for her. Just then, Sheetal joked that Zara had to put on weight before thinking of buying it and took it from her. Then the maid came in with a tray filled with bowls of piping hot soup for everyone. I was very alert now as the maid represented a risk factor. But there was no incident. She quietly served everyone and left. As she was leaving, my eyes automatically looked for the ring and saw that it was safe in Sheetal's hand. She asked me if she could try it on and take a photo. Guiltily remembering how I had done it, I asked the young girl to go ahead".

"There was only one maid, I guess. Was the food catered or cooked on the premises?" Radha wanted to know.

"Yes, only one maid. She has been working with the Mulchandanis since many years. She is a very good cook and since it was only seven of us, she had done the cooking herself".

Tara stopped only for a sip of water. "Sheetal wore the ring and tried to take a photo but because the curtains were drawn, there was less light. So she went to the window and asked Hema to take the picture. Minal, Zara and I too joined them near the window with our soup bowls. Just as Hema was about to click, Sheetal asked her to wait as she wanted the ring on her left hand and was pulling it off her finger when Minal tripped on the carpet suddenly. She fell down, throwing some of the hot soup on her own pure white and gold sari, a lot on Zara and a little on Sheetal's feet. Everyone was around, trying to help Minal up, using tissues to wipe the soup off Zara. Minal had rushed to the wash basin in the same room and was trying to wash the red stains off her sari. Suddenly, Sheetal cried out aloud that she couldn't find the ring".

"What did she say about it"?

"She said she was sure she had kept it on the table nearby and bent to check her burning toes. But when everyone was settled, it had simply vanished".

"What about Nancy and Vimala? You didn't mention anything about them when all of you were near the window".

"Smart of you to realize that. Nancy has a rather bad name. There have been a couple of other incidents when things have gone missing when she was around. So I had asked Vimala to keep an eye on her as I did not want to lose my precious ring. So Vimala was with her on the sofa when we were all at the window. When the commotion happened, both of them got up and were trying to help. Vimala isn't very sure, but she thinks Nancy had suddenly walked away from the group and went to her handbag lying near the sofa".

"Did you ask her why she left the group and did not help to clean the mess?"

"Yes. She said she felt there was a call on her mobile and had gone to check".

"You must have checked her handbag?"

"Of course! Sheetal was totally upset, as the ring was with her when it disappeared. So she insisted that firstly she and then everyone be searched in person and their handbags too. So I first checked Hema, whom I did not even doubt. Then both of us together searched everyone thoroughly. We looked in everyone's handbags too. No trace of it. I can say with confidence it was not there in the whole room. It had simply vanished".

"Did the maid enter the room anytime again?"

"Definitely not. I have racked my brains 100 times after that and also we all talked about it. The ring was very much there after the maid left and she never came back".

"Is there some way it could have been handed to someone outside the window?"

"The flat is on the 34th floor. I first checked if it is stuck somewhere outside the window. It wasn't there. Next, I went into the washroom and called my driver secretly and asked him to go and check the area right under the window. He reported that anything thrown from the window would fall outside the apartment compound into a wasteland filled with garbage. No one can find a ring there. The area is cordoned off by a spiked fence all around and no one could have stood there expecting the ring to fall too".

Tara checked Radha's face and said, "I know it's baffling. I will understand if you can't find out. I was not very hopeful, but since Vimala was very confident about you, I thought I would just try. Anyway thank you for hearing me out".

"But I know who did it and how".

"What!" Tara couldn't believe her ears.

"Yes. I'll tell you right now and you can go and tell them that this is how it was done and you will go to the police. The culprits will quietly hand it over to you".

Radha continued, "As you yourself could have guessed, the whole soup dropping had to be set up so that there would be confusion. As Minal had dropped it, she must have been a part of the plan. Once that is understood, everything else falls into place. She must have planned the whole thing as soon as she saw the picture of the ring you sent. She must have got a similar one made which wouldn't have stood scrutiny but could pass off as the original from far. Just think back. After Sheetal got the ring, no one else handled it and it was always hidden in her hand. So when the maid came in with the soup tray, Sheetal must have used her chewing gum to stick it below the tray. The maid, who also was in on the plan, just took it away in front of everyone's eyes. Sheetal had the imitation one all along and staged wanting a picture with the ring. When Minal dropped the soup on purpose, and everyone was looking at the stain on her white sari, Sheetal must have thrown it out of the window and continued to make a fuss about her burnt toes. How much ever you searched, you couldn't have found it anywhere. By then the maid must have taken the original out of the house".

❋❋❋

Next day, there was a beautiful bouquet on Radha's table with a 'THANK YOU' card in it.